BOOKS BY SHANNON HALE

THE BOOKS OF BAYERN:

The Goose Girl

Enna Burning

River Secrets

Forest Born

Princess Academy

Book of a Thousand Days

GRAPHIC NOVELS:
with Dean Hale
illustrations by Nathan Hale

Rapunzel's Revenge

Calamity Jack

FOR ADULTS:

Austenland

The Actor and the Housewife

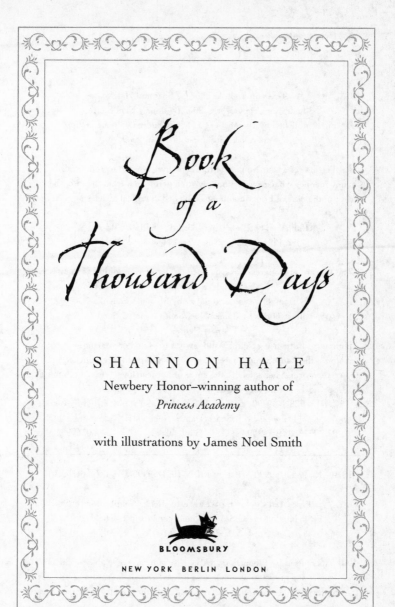

Book of a Thousand Days

SHANNON HALE

Newbery Honor–winning author of
Princess Academy

with illustrations by James Noel Smith

BLOOMSBURY

NEW YORK BERLIN LONDON

Text copyright © 2007 by Shannon Hale
Illustrations copyright © 2007 by James Noel Smith
First published by Bloomsbury U.S.A. Children's Books in 2007
Paperback edition published in 2009

Published by Bloomsbury U.S.A. Children's Books
175 Fifth Avenue, New York, New York 10010

The Library of Congress has cataloged the hardcover edition as follows:
Hale, Shannon.
Book of a thousand days / by Shannon Hale ;
illustrations by James Noel Smith. —1st U.S. ed.
p.   cm.
Summary: Fifteen-year-old Dashti, sworn to obey her sixteen-year-old
mistress, the Lady Saren, shares Saren's years of punishment locked in a
tower, then brings her safely to the lands of her true love, where both must
hide who they are as they work as kitchen maids.
ISBN-13: 978-1-59990-051-3 • ISBN-10: 1-59990-051-3 (hardcover)
[1. Fantasy.] I. Smith, James Noel, ill. II. Title.
PZ7.H13824Boo 2007   [Fic]—dc22   2006036999

ISBN-13: 978-1-59990-378-1 • ISBN-10: 1-59990-378-4 (paperback)

Typeset in Cochin by Westchester Book Composition
Printed in the U.S.A. by Quebecor World Fairfield
1 3 5 7 9 10 8 6 4 2

FOR VICTORIA

To the girl and the geese nine others said, Nay!
But you poured me some tea and asked me to stay
And built me a cottage at Bloomsbury Place
With pillows on chairs and sun on my face.
Our fifth together is me hugging you;
May dozens more follow before we are through.

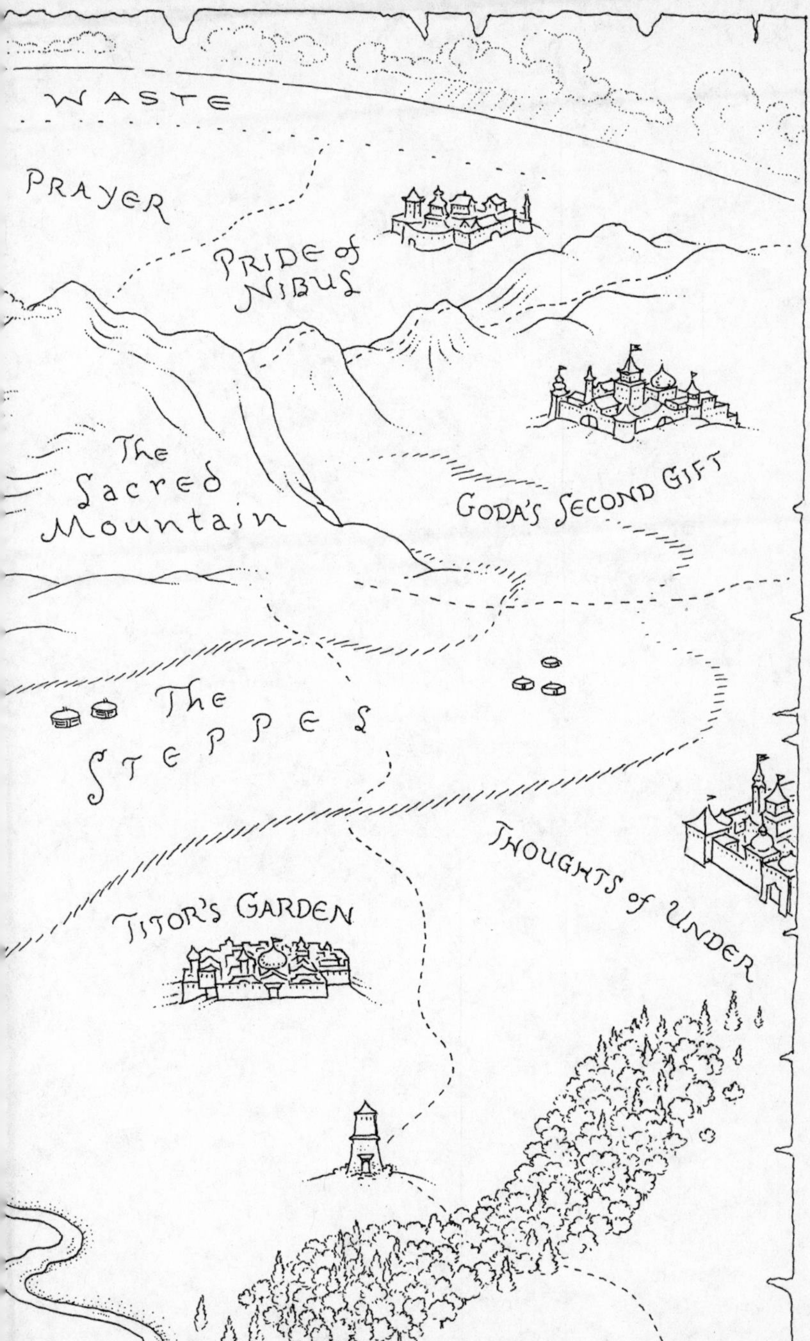

WASTE

PRAYER

PRIDE of NIBUS

The Sacred Mountain

GODA'S SECOND GIFT

The STEPPES

THOUGHTS of UNDER

TITOR'S GARDEN

A book of thoughts kept by Dashti,

a mucker and a lady's maid,

Containing an account of our seven years

in a tower and our adventure thereafter

PART 1

The Tower

Day 1

My lady and I are being shut up in a tower for seven years.

Lady Saren is sitting on the floor, staring at the wall, and hasn't moved even to scratch for an hour or more. Poor thing. It's a shame I don't have fresh yak dung or anything strong-smelling to scare the misery out of her.

The men are bricking up the door, and I hear them muttering and scraping cement. Only a small square of unbricked sky and light still gape at me. I smile back at its mean grin to show I'm not scared. Isn't it something, all the trouble they're going to for us? I feel like a jewel in a treasure box, though my lady is the —

My lady suddenly awoke from her stupor and sprang at the door, clawing at the bricks, trying to shove her way out. How she screamed! Like an angry piglet.

"Stay in!" we heard her honored father say. He

must have been standing near the opening. "Stay until your heart softens like long-boiled potatoes. And if you try to break your way out, I've told the guards to kill you on sight. You have seven years to think about disobedience. Until you are meek with regret, your face turns my stomach."

I nearly warned him that such words would bring him bad luck and canker his own heart. Thank the Ancestors that my lady's fit stopped me from speaking out of turn. When I pulled her back, her hands were red from beating at the bricks and streaked with wet cement. This isn't exactly a happy-celebration morning, but I don't see what good it does to thrash about.

"Easy, my lady," I said, the way I'd speak to a feisty ram. It wasn't too hard to hold my lady back, even squirming as she was. I'm fifteen years, and though skinny as a skinned hare, I'm strong as a yak, or so my mama used to say. I sang the calming song, the one that goes, "Oh, moth on a wind, oh, leaf on a stream," and invites the hearer into dreaming. I feared my lady was so angry she wouldn't heed the song. But she must've been eager to sleep, because now she's snoring on my lap. Happily the brush and ink are at hand so I can keep writing. When you can't move, there isn't much to do but think, and I don't much want to think right now.

Sticky sobs shake my lady even while she sleeps. My own eyes are heavy. Perhaps it's the darkness making us so drowsy. Goda, goddess of sleep, keep us tonight.

Day 2

It's quiet and as dark as night, our only light a quivering candle. The door is bricked solid. From time to time I hear voices, so I suppose the guards remain outside.

Goda heard my prayer last night and did let us sleep until morning. I know it's morning because I peeked through the dump hole. That's a tiny metal flap that opens just enough to empty our chamber pot and wash water on the ground outside. It looks like this.

When I push it open, a lip of brick wall prevents me from looking straight out, but I can see the ground five handspans down. Very thoughtful of her honored father, I think, to design our prison such, so we have a way to throw out our waste and don't have to breathe foul air for seven years.

This tower used to be a lookout tower, standing as it does on the border between Titor's Garden, which is her honored father's land, and Thoughts of Under, which is the realm to the east. The upper story was the lookout, but the windows are bricked blind now. Too easy to escape from, I suppose, or else her honored father hopes to crush her spirits with darkness. The upper floor is my lady's chamber. The air is best there because tiny slits in the bricks let fresh air slink in. If I press my face to a certain slit, I think I can see blue that is the sky. Or maybe I'm just seeing shadows.

The middle story is our kitchen, with hearth, pots, table, and one chair. Stacks and stacks of wood line the walls, and my own straw mattress keeps the floor company. A ladder descends into the cellar. It looks something like this.

And here's the bit that makes me tremble with delight—in our cellar there is a mountain of food! Barrels and bags and crates of it. And we have a fine well dug right in the cellar floor. My lady is napping in her chamber, so I just came down here to look at the food. Seven years' worth. Such a thing I never imagined. Even though I can't see the sky, it's hard not to want to dance about, knowing that for seven years at least I won't starve. That's paradise for a mucker like me. How my mama would laugh.

Day 6

I've been much occupied these past days, learning the ways of our tower, counting sacks of flour and rice, barrels of dried and salted mutton, figuring how much we may eat each day and last for seven years. It's useful knowing my letters and numbers so I can write down the figuring. We've boxes of candles and a stack of parchment, surely enough to keep me writing for seven years.

These are the meals I've cooked these last days:

Breakfast—warmed milk with sugar, eaten with flat barley cakes. Each morning the guards knock on the metal flap and hand up a horn of fresh mare's milk. First thing, I splash a drop of milk in the north corner, facing the direction of the Sacred Mountain, and say my prayers. By tradition, I should dribble the milk on soil, not stones, but it'll have to do since the metal flap faces south.

Dinner—dung cakes. That's what we muckers call them, though I don't use that crude term around my lady, of course. They're made of salted meat (simmered long to soften) and onions, wrapped in dough and cooked on coals. That's how we used to eat them with Mama, only here I get to add spices— cinnamon and peppercorns! Two times before the tower I'd eaten spiced food, but never had I reached my own hand into a barrel and touched the raw powders and seeds. Someday when I leave this life and my soul climbs the Sacred Mountain, I imagine the Ancestors will be too beautiful and bright to look at, but their skin and breath will smell of peppercorns and cinnamon, anise, cardamom, and fennel. Heavenly, it is.

Supper—rice and dried peas, boiled with milk and raisins, and sweetened with a pinch of sugar. Delicious. My lady says she's used to eating the large meal at night instead of midday, but that makes no sense to me. She didn't order me to change the dinner and supper order, so I'll keep it the same.

These past meals have been as hearty as I ever had, and if being a lady's maid means I get to eat the same food as my lady—with spices even!—then you'll never hear me complain.

Sometimes to get her through a long day, I give my lady a mess of dried fruit or a slap of cheese. Even so, she swears she's starving. The mouth grumbles more than the stomach, my mama used to say. My lady can't really be hungry—I think she's just sad to be imprisoned away from her love and hoping that the food will fill her up where her heart breaks.

But so much food! Each day we eat three times, and I roll around on my mattress at night and laugh into my arm and pray to my mama so she knows I'm doing fine.

Day 11

It occurs to me I ought to relate the why behind our imprisonment. And at the moment, with dinner eaten and cleaned up, washing done, and my lady resting, I've nothing more to do but stare at the candle flame. It tosses and bobs like a spring foal and sometimes I find myself staring at it so long, the flame is all I can see for an hour after. But now I'll write.

I came to the city of Titor's Garden only one year ago. My mother, the Ancestors bless her, died from the floating fevers that take people in the summer. I was alone, my father dead when I was a baby, and my brothers gone to make their world way when I was a girl of eight and still in two braids. I wear one braid now, though still long down my back. My lady wears her braid pinned up, though she's not married and just one year older than me. I suppose she has the right to do her hair how she pleases, her being gentry and all.

Anyway, with my mother passed to the Ancestors' Realm, I made the long walk from the summer pastures to the city, hoping to find work. The city had too many people for my mind. Where do they all sleep? How do you feed so many bodies? My head hurt trying to reason it out. I found the house of chiefs soon enough and purchased employment with my last animal. A thin woman people named "Mistress" had me stand before her and tell what skills I had, declaring at the end that I would be of best use working in the stables. When she rose from her chair to show me the way, she winced and rubbed her back.

"Have a pain there, Mistress?" I asked.

She didn't answer. I suppose it was right nosy of me to speak up like that, but I thought I could help her, and why sit quiet when you can be useful? So I said, "I might help that pain, Mistress, if you let me."

She didn't argue, so I put my hand on her back and I started with the song for body aches, the slow, sliding tune that goes, "Tell me again, how does it go?" and then twined into it the hopping tune for buried pain that goes, "Berries in summer, red, purple, green."

She stretched when I was finished. "You're a mucker, then? I've heard of the healing songs but never thought much about them." She looked at me thoughtfully, then set in on any number of queer questions.

"What is the proper remedy for a lady in fits?"

"Make her drink warm milk and rub her back," I answered easily enough.

"Show me a straight stitch."

9

And I sewed a line straighter than the finger of Ris, god of roads and towns.

"Let me see your hands," she said, and checked them for calluses. "Mmm-hmm. And your mucker mother taught you all the healing songs?"

"I don't think a body can know them all, but I know the useful ones, like the song for helping a mare birth a foal and the song to get a she-yak to stand still for milking—"

"No, no, I have no use for horses and yaks. The songs for aches of back and belly and head. Like you just sang for me."

"I know dozens, I guess."

"Then I'm going to make you a lady's maid for the most honored house in Titor's Garden. Our lord's second daughter, Lady Saren, she's bound to need a fresh maid by the time your education is done. She certainly seems to go through them quickly."

Mistress sent me to an old man named Qadan, who lived beside the house of chiefs. I cooked and cleaned for him, and in the afternoons, a group of hopeful scribes joined us for lessons in reading.

"As Lady Saren's maid you'll need to know your letters," Mistress had said. I didn't know then why this is so, but I do now—because unlike most gentry, Lady Saren herself doesn't know them.

What a strange and wondrous time it was, eating two big meals every single day, sleeping by a fire always lit, and learning the secret language of ink strokes. On days when I finished chores and errands early, Qadan taught me sketching. I was so busy and my belly so full, I would fall asleep even as I was falling into bed.

But some nights, when I tossed on my mattress, awake and staring at nothing, the sorrow would strike me. Quiet there in Qadan's dark house, my heartache felt like a river, and I was sinking into it, carried away fast in its coldness. That's the best way I can explain it, and what I mean by it is, I missed my mama.

Sometimes Qadan threw candlesticks at us when his back pinched him sour, but mostly he was a good teacher. He said the best way to practice writing was to keep a book of thoughts. The first one I wrote in was left behind in our rush to this prison. I found this blank book of stitched-together pages among the parchment and inks, and I asked my lady if I might take it for my own. She had no use for it.

It seems a bit of a laugh now, all that time spent learning and now I find myself in a tower with no occasion to write my lady's love letters or keep her books. Instead I'll record the details of our confinement, so when the seven years are over and the lord's men pound through the walls, if all they find is a delicate lady and her humble maid shriveled like old ginger roots from lack of sun and air, they'll know somewhat of our happy time still breathing.

Though my lady doesn't sound happy. She's thrashing on her mattress again. I wonder, is it in the gentry's nature to suffer so? Could the Ancestors give gentry beauty and perfection, food and large houses, and a world to do their bidding, and yet curse them with wretched sorrow? My poor, poor lady.

I had best go see to her now and finish my account later. There will be, I'd guess, plenty of time to do so.

Day 13

While I was washing up tonight, my lady fell asleep on my mattress, not wanting to climb to her chamber. She wears fashionable shoes with the toe long and curled toward her ankle, which are certainly pretty but do make it difficult to clamber up ladders. It wouldn't be proper for me to sleep on her mattress, so I'll finish my story before making my bed of the grain sacks in the cellar. The Ancestors bless her.

After one year with Qadan, Mistress had me take the oath of a lady's maid. I cut my finger, splashed drops of blood toward the north and the Sacred Mountain, and swore to serve the gentry and my new mistress however the Ancestors saw fit.

"But I'm still a mucker, right?" I asked.

"You'll always be a mucker," said Mistress.

I was relieved. I know muckers are the simplest of commoners and becoming a lady's maid is a right honor, but I couldn't give up the wild steppes forever, couldn't turn my back on Mama and all she taught. I feel like a mucker from the ends of my hair to the mud of my bones.

After the oath, Mistress escorted me to the city's center and left me at the lord's house. It was near as beautiful as a mountain in autumn with its three-tiered roof covered in red and green enamel tiles. Inside was less welcoming—grand and cold, the floor stones seemingly cut from ice. Everyone was running around, women were wailing, men were yelling. At the time, I thought it was always that way. I hadn't heard yet of the trouble.

Hours I spent sitting in a corner, waiting for someone to be sensible. I could see myself in a mirror, and I stared and thought how plain I looked in my mucker boots and working clothes inside a gentry's house as fine as sugar. I'll sketch it from memory, so it won't be just right.

No one paid me the least mind, and though it wasn't proper, I decided I'd find my new mistress myself. Ancestors forgive me, but what else could I do? I was of no use to anyone just sitting there.

Errand boys rushed up and down corridors, maidens sulked on benches. Some wept. When I asked for directions to Lady Saren's chamber, no one questioned why I wished to go there.

I entered the chamber slowly, squinting. I'd never met any gentry before and was worried that the glory of the Ancestors might be so bright inside her, it would burn my eyes. I was a little disappointed then to find my lady looking much like anyone else, still in her white sleep clothes, her hair in a braid with half the hair poking out. Her eyes were puffy and red, her nose wet, her feet bare. She sat on her bed, alone, straight as a tent pole.

The first thing I wanted to do was comb her hair straight and plait it tight, dress her and set her up like a proper lady, let the glory of her divine ancestors shine in her properly. But I had to stand there, quiet, and wait for her to look up and see me. It isn't allowed for a commoner, of course, to speak to gentry first.

The flats of my feet were aching by the time she saw. And in all that time she hadn't moved.

"Who are you?" she asked. There was something about her manner that reminded me of a little girl, though I learned since that she's sixteen years.

"My lady, I'm Dashti. I'm your new maid."

"You can't be, they're all hiding from me because they don't want—" She considered me. "What is your name?"

"Dashti, my lady," I told her again.

She hopped off her bed and grabbed my wrist, but tight. Her swiftness and force startled me. "Swear you'll serve me, Dashti. Swear you won't abandon me. Swear it!"

"Of course, my lady, I swear." I didn't know why she grabbed me and yelled. I'd already taken the oath and learned to write letters and everything.

"All right," she said, wandering around the room as if looking for something. "All right then."

I led her back to the bed and had her sit while I combed the muddle of her hair and bound it in a braid, every hair crisscrossing so the smarts wouldn't wander out of her head. She scarcely moved as I washed her face and hands and underarms and feet.

I looked in her wardrobe for clothing and found two dozen deels. They were like the long-sleeved robes over tunic and trousers that any commoner wears, but they resembled my own deel as much as a worm resembles a snake. Before coming to the city, the only cloth I'd seen was leather, fur, or felt. Qadan taught me the names of other cloths—brocade, satin, damask, silk. My lady had them all, I'd dare guess, and embroidered and fine, layers stitched upon each other, trimmed and as colorful as a summer sunset. You must think I fib, claiming any person could have such clothes and so many, but I swear by the eight Ancestors that I speak true as truth.

When she was dressed and combed and cleaned, the beauty that is Lady Saren really began to show, and I think she felt it, too. Once she even said, "Thank you, Dashti."

Those words made me feel combed and cleaned myself.

Then her honored father entered, and she stiffened and began to whimper as if fighting off a fit of sobs. He had one crooked leg. This surprised me fit to staring. I don't mean disrespect, but I'd always thought that gentry would be formed and perfect of limb, lovely and radiant, being the offspring of the Ancestors. But truth be, if her father had worn common clothing, I might've thought him a mucker. Either the Ancestors want it this way, or else Under, god of tricks, was deceiving my eyes.

"Still bleating about it, are you?" said her honored father. He was a man too small for his voice. "Titor and his dogs, girl—it's your mess. Crying about it is like rolling around in your own filth."

He watched her for a moment, and I swear by Titor *and* his dogs that there was a touch of sympathy in his eyes. I'd have sworn it on my mother's memory till he up and slapped her face. It didn't make sense, as though he slapped her more from duty than anger.

Mama used to say, "Hitting is the language of cowards and drunkards," and here a member of the honored gentry struck his daughter for crying.

"What's this thing here?" he asked, looking at me now, taking in my rough boots, my wool deel, my leather sash. "Why is one of your maids dressed as a mucker? Are you a mucker? Answer me, girl."

I answered him. "Yes, my lord, I was born on the steppes, and when I came to my lord's city last year I—"

"That's enough, I don't want the whole story. You're nothing to look at, are you?"

I thought that was a useless question. I'm right aware of the red birth splotches on my face and arm, not to mention my dull hair and lips thinner than the edge of a leaf. Mama said that beauty is a curse for muckers. She once told me about Bayar, her clan sister, who looked like Evela, goddess of sunlight. And what happened to Bayar? A lord fell for her beauty, got her with child, then left both girl and baby in the mud and never returned. That's gentry's right, I guess, but it was a bit hard on Bayar.

"I remember now," my lady's father said with a *humph*, "Mistress Tolui said some mucker girl was coming from Qadan's. What a hell you walked into, though it can't be worse than your own home. Muckers survive on grass alone, just like sheep, isn't that right?"

"Well, my lord," I said, not sure how to contradict gentry, "we—"

He slapped his daughter's face again, suddenly and with no cause, like a snake striking. The sound of her cry was sharp and sad enough to break a bird's wing. It was then that I began to understand my lady — I think she must've lost her mother long ago, before she was old enough to learn how to comfort herself.

"There she goes again!" he said, his big voice booming out of his small head. "She'd gone quiet, and I've grown accustomed to her crying. Bawl all you want, wench! No one will hear you alone in the tower."

At that, she forced her tears to stop and looked right back at him, as brave as anything I've seen. "I won't be alone," she said. "My new maid is going with me."

"Is that what you think?" He was rummaging through her wardrobe, pulling deels from their hooks and tossing them onto the floor. "You don't deserve a maid, and I won't force one to attend you. So let me hear the maid say she's willing to go."

My lady was clinging to my arm.

"Go where?" I asked.

Her father laughed. "Now I understand." He took hold of one of the deels and ripped the sleeves off. "I, her honored father, have arranged an enviable match with Lord Khasar. He is the lord of Thoughts of Under, the most powerful of the Eight Realms. And does my daughter thank me? And appreciate her responsibility to form this alliance? No, she declares she's promised herself to Khan Tegus of the lesser realm Song for Evela. She refuses to marry Lord Khasar. How's that for gratitude? I'm sending her to a watchtower shut up as a prison and we'll see if seven years beneath bricks won't kill her rebellion. So say it, mucker girl, will you lock yourself up with this disobedient child?"

My lady was squeezing my arm so tightly now, my fingers felt cold. One of her cheeks was pink from his slap, her brown eyes red from crying. She reminded me of a lamb just tumbled out, wet all over, unsure of her feet and suspicious of the sun.

She'd be alone in that tower, I thought, and I remembered our tent after Mama died, how the air seemed to have gone out of it, how the walls leaned in, like to bury me dead. When Mama left, what had been home became just a heap of sticks and felt. It's not good being alone like that. Not good.

Besides, I'd sworn to serve my mistress. And now that her hair was fixed and her face washed, I saw just how lovely she was, the glory of the Ancestors shining through her. I felt certain that Lady Saren would never disobey her father lightly. Surely she had a wise and profound reason for stubbornness, one blessed by the Ancestors.

"Yes," I said. "I'll stay with my lady."

Then her father up and slapped me across my mouth. It almost made me laugh.

I'm right proud of myself for remembering so much! Maybe I got a few words wrong, but that's so near how the conversation went, I'm going to call it truth. My hand aches from writing and my ink grows thin from watering, so I'll finish for tonight.

Day 14

As my lady didn't budge from my mattress last night, I slept as I could on the sacks of barley flour in the cellar, but squeaks and scratches kept nipping at my dreams. When I woke from a nightmare and sat up, two tiny eyes stared back.

A rat. And where there's one, there must be more.

This makes me count numbers and rub my forehead. There's seven years of food for my lady and her maid. We don't have enough to spare for a family of rats. I found four sacks of grain with holes nibbled through and counted six tallow candles missing from a box. What if they eat more? A lot more? How will we survive seven years with rat-spoiled food and no light?

Day 19

Little time for writing these past days. When I'm not washing and cooking or singing and caring for my lady, I sit in the cellar with the broom and swat at anything with eyes. There are a dozen rats at least.

I don't have arsenic to make rat bread, so I fashioned a trap the best I could. Among our supplies I found some nails, as long as my finger and sharp, too. I drove them up through the lid of a barrel then lay atop the nails a piece of parchment. It looked a solid object to me, and to the rat as well, I suppose. Here's how it must've been:

I found it this morning, its body stuck inside the spikes with one nail up through its chin. I won't show it to my lady, save her. She is already feeling ill. I sang the song for stomachache but she grew tired of the melody and sent me away. I hear her upstairs rocking on her bed.

Sometimes I think there's something not quite right with my lady. She seems sad, but when I sing the song for sadness, she doesn't respond. Nor does the song for clear thoughts make her think straight. I guess a couple of songs just isn't going to be enough for whatever ails her. Mistress chose me because I know the songs, and now I begin to realize that my duty with Lady Saren will be more than just keeping her fed and clean. Perhaps the Ancestors sent me to heal her.

But what ails her? Could it just be she's that heartsick for her love, Khan Tegus? I can't wrap my thoughts around how deep their love must be. It's too high above me. It's surely a powerful love that bids a girl brick herself away from the Eternal Blue Sky for seven years. I once liked a boy named Yeke with kind eyes, but I wouldn't have given up the sun for him. Her khan must be such a man from legend, a man formed by Evela, goddess of sunlight. Perhaps if I looked at him, I'd have to squint. I'll ask my lady.

Later

My lady doesn't recall squinting.

Day 27

Not only have I been unsuccessful so far in healing my lady, she seems to have worsened. She spooks at sudden noises, like the wind getting hooked in the chimney or the wood floor whining under my feet. She startles and cries out as if each new sound were a cold hand grabbing her from behind.

Today while she lay upstairs, I heard a voice shouting outside, and I thought, Ancestors preserve us, but my lady's not going to like that. Sure enough, she poured herself down the ladder so fast, she fell to her knees at the bottom. Not waiting to stand again, she crawled to me and clutched my legs.

"He's here, Dashti. Do something! He's here!"

I didn't know who she meant. I was certain the voice had been one of the guards who circles our tower, and I told her so.

"No, it's him, it's him."

"Who, my lady?"

"It's Lord Khasar." She stared at the walls as if expecting them to fall down around her. "He'll be furious that I refused him. He won't give up. I knew he wouldn't. In this tower, I'm a tethered goat left out for the wolf, and now he'll take me and marry me and kill me."

I held her and sang to her and let our dinner burn on the fire, and all the while she shook and cried dry tears, her mouth hanging open. I've never seen a person cry like that, with real fear. She made my blood shiver. I wish I knew what ails her, but perhaps it's too soon. Mama used to say, you have to know someone a thousand days before you can glimpse her soul. When the chill in the stones told us it was night, my lady's grip relaxed. She was so tired from shaking, she fell asleep on my mattress. I guess I'll be sleeping in the cellar with the rats.

I wonder what it is about Lord Khasar that makes her tremble fit to come apart at the joints. And I wonder if he really will come for her. But there's no sense in worrying about it. If he does come, we've nowhere to run.

Day 31

A few minutes ago we heard a voice. I dropped the robe I was washing and hurried to my lady, who clasped me so tightly around my neck I couldn't talk.

"It's him, it's him," she muttered, hiding her face in my neck. "I told you! It's Khasar and he's come back."

But then I really listened. The voice became clearer, and I heard it calling in a hush, "Lady Saren! Can you hear me? It's Tegus. My lady, I'm so sorry."

I gasped. "My lady! It's your khan—it's Khan Tegus!"

She stared at the wall. I expected her to run forward and cry for happiness to hear his voice, but she didn't move. Even now as I write this, my lady sits on my mattress, hugging her knees to her chest. And her khan continues to call.

"Go to him," I say. "You can talk through the flap."

But she just shakes her head.

Later

I'll do my best to remember exactly how it went.

It didn't seem right to keep her poor khan calling, his voice rasping in an effort to whisper and shout at once. Someone should answer at least. I fetched a wooden spoon and lodged it against the flap to hold it open.

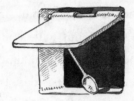

I was just about to speak when my lady leaped at me, covering my mouth with her hand.

"What will you say?" she whispered.

"What would you like me to say?" I asked under her fingers.

My lady removed her hand and started to pace and fret and rub her head. She looked as if she'd like to run away, had there been anywhere to run. My poor lady.

"Say you are me."

"What? But why, my lady?"

"You are my maid, Dashti," she said, and though

27

she still shook like a rabbit, her voice was hard and full of the knowledge that she's gentry. "It is my right to have my maid speak for me. I don't like to speak to someone directly. What if it isn't really him? What if he means us harm?"

"But he'll know my voice isn't yours, and if he knows—"

My lady raised her hand and commanded me to obey on the sacred nine—the eight Ancestors and the Eternal Blue Sky. It's a sin most gruesome to play at being what you're not, and worse than sin to be a commoner speaking as a lady, but what could I do when she commanded me on the sacred nine? She is my mistress and an honored lady besides. I never should have argued. The Ancestors forgive me.

"Khan . . . Khan Tegus," I said through the hole. I stuttered hideously, my words mimicking my scattered heartbeat. "I'm here. Sss—Saren."

I could hear him come closer, and by moonlight, I saw the tip of his boot step on that patch of ground beneath the flap. I thought to be grateful rain had come that morning and the ground was clean.

"My lady, I am so sorry. I came to Titor's Garden to reason with your father, but he wouldn't attend me. His message said only that you are to wed Lord Khasar or no one. I've counseled with my war chief and he says if we attack your father outright, we have a good hope of winning, but we'll incur terrible fatalities on both sides. I thought . . . I imagined you wouldn't want me to do that. I would hate to face your own father and brother in battle."

"No, of course not," I said. His voice sounded so sad, I tried to think of something to cheer him. "Don't worry, we have loads of food, even five bags of sugar and enough dried yogurt to keep a sow and all her sisters happy."

Her khan laughed, sounding surprised to be laughing at all. "That's good news."

"Isn't it? We've fifteen bags of wheat flour, twenty bags of barley, forty-two barrels of salted mutton . . . well, you don't want to hear all about our food."

"And why not? What's better than food?"

"Exactly!" I thought her khan showed good taste and was much more interesting now that his voice had ceased to be so plaintive. "But how are you able to talk to us? Do our guards know you're here?"

"They're asleep," he said. "My men are camped in the woods near here, and I've been watching for hours until all your guards went into their tents to warm themselves. The night's pressing cold. A guard may peek around again, so I shouldn't stay long, but I'll return tomorrow. Is there anything that you need?"

What did my lady need? Sunlight, starlight, fresh air. I said, "Something from outside, perhaps? A flower would be lovely to see."

"A flower? I thought you might want something more than that."

I didn't want to complain about the rats, I wasn't sure if gentry would, so I just said, "We have plenty of food and blankets. We're fine."

"I'm relieved. Farewell until tomorrow, my lady."

"Farewell. . . ." I found I didn't dare say "my lord" in return. It was too much a lie. He is *her* lord, *her* khan. Feeling as though I had swallowed a great lump of knotted rope, I brought in the wooden spoon, letting the flap clank shut. Immediately I knelt facing north and prayed, "Ancestors, forgive me, Dashti, a mucker, for lying in words and deeds."

I said it aloud and hoped my prayer would prick my lady a little, so next time she'd speak to her khan on her own.

Why is she so afraid? It makes no sense. She gets worse every day, I think. Perhaps she's tower-addled. I'll go comb her hair and sing the song again for setting a person's brains straight, the one that goes, "Under, over, down, and through, light in the big house, food on the table."

Day 32

He came again last night, whisper-shouting, "My lady! My lady!"

That's not me, so I didn't answer. I stayed on my mattress, mending a stocking, wishing on each stitch that my lady would go speak to her khan herself.

"My lady?" He tapped on the metal flap. It can't be opened from the outside. *Rap, rap, rap.* "Lady Saren? Are you all right?"

At last she arose from our one chair and stood before me. I kept stitching, praying she would act.

"Speak with him, Dashti," she said.

"Please, my lady . . ." I shouldn't have argued, Mistress would've scolded, but better to be scolded than hanged on the city's south wall. In the city, I learned that's where they execute those whose crimes are so rotten they'd have no hope of ascending into the Ancestors' Realm. The south wall. The wall farthest from the Sacred Mountain.

My lady offered me her hand. How perfect her hands are! I've never seen skin like hers, so soft, no rough spots on her fingertips, her palms like the underside of calf leather. She'll be made to touch nothing harder than water, so I swore by the eight Ancestors and the Eternal Blue Sky. And if what she commands leads my head into a neck rope, then so be my lady's will.

I spoke a prayer in my heart—*Pardon me, Nibus, god of order.*

She sat on my mattress while I lodged the wooden spoon beneath the flap.

"I'm here," I said. I could see his boot in the puddle of moonlight. It was brown leather, double stitched. It would take a mucker a week to make one of those boots.

"I didn't wake you?" he asked.

"Oh, no, I never sleep. . . ." I was going to say that I never sleep until my lady does, but I stopped myself.

"You never sleep?"

"No, yes, I do, I just, I mean . . ." I don't know how to lie to gentry.

"That's a shame. I'll say some prayers for you to Goda, goddess of sleep."

His voice went dry. I knew he was teasing me, so I said, "And I'll pray for you to Carthen, goddess of strength. Your ankles look too skinny to carry you." They didn't, of course, but accusing one of having skinny ankles is a friendly insult among muckers, and it felt so natural to say.

I could hear the smile in his voice when he said, "I'll wager it'd take three of your ankles to make one of mine."

"Not a chance," I said. "I have sturdy ankles, strong as tree trunks."

"Show me, then."

So I did. I was wearing a pair of my lady's older slippers, the kind with the toe curled up prettily, so I was proud to let him see my foot when I lowered my right leg through the flap down to my knee. I could feel her khan press his own leg against mine, measuring our ankles together.

"Hmm," he said, "I hate to contradict, my lady, but I think my ankle puts yours to shame."

"Not a chance. And it's not a fair comparison, as you're wearing boots." I was giggling. I couldn't help it, it was so ridiculous, my leg down the dump hole to prove I had sturdy ankles, her khan measuring them, and my lady surely wondering if we're insane. And then when I tried to lift my leg back up, I got stuck, and I felt his hands unhook the tip of my slipper from a metal catch and help raise my leg. He was chuckling by now, too.

"Oh! I brought you a gift."

He lifted something. He used both hands as one does to show deep respect. I thought how he must have had to kneel on the ground to do so. I thought how no one had ever offered me something with both hands before.

It was a pine bough. I reached down and took it. His hands were cold and rough, and I wished I'd had gloves to give him. I thought to hold his hand and sing the song for warmth, but that wouldn't do at all, a mucker holding gentry's hand, and him thinking me his betrothed lady. Not at all.

"You asked for a flower," he said, "but in autumn there's little to choose from. Besides, I think pine boughs smell better, don't you?"

I smelled it like I was starving and the odor alone would fill up my belly. My head got dizzy with memories of Mama and being cold and cozy.

"It smells like the winter nap," I said, longing for some truth to tell. "Midwinter every year, my mother would decorate our . . . our home with pine boughs, cracking the needles to get the richest smell, then we'd curl up in blankets and take our winter nap, five days of no food but milk, sleeping on and off all day and night, like the burrowing animals do."

"That sounds strange and lovely and wearying, too. Is winter nap a common custom in Titor's Garden?"

"Common enough." I didn't say that it's common for muckers. We do it as a prayer to Vera, goddess of food, to help us through another year, and we do it because at midwinter there's not much food for the having anyway. I don't suppose my lady needed a winter nap, with her honored father's cellars full of grain.

"In Song for Evela, our midwinter rite is just the opposite. All folk come together under my roof and eat and eat and eat. Enough cakes, apples, mutton, and raisin rice to last a year! Sometimes it feels good to feast until it hurts."

"You feast with muckers, even?"

"What are muckers?"

"The folk that live on the grassy steppes in ghers—those are felt tents they make themselves."

"Are they herding folk?"

"That's right. The steppes of Titor's Garden are too hard for farming, rocky and windy and rough. Muckers do work when work is sent out from the city folk, and the rest of the time they travel with the seasons, herding sheep, horses, reindeer, yaks."

"May I say something? Will you be offended?"

"No . . . ," I said, though I was thinking, He knows I'm a mucker!

But then he said, "Your hand, when you took my pine bough, I saw—your hand is beautiful."

I tucked my hands under my arms and looked

35

at my lady. She was staring at her own hands and frowning. All I could think was, thank the Ancestors that I took the bough with my right hand and not my left, which bears the red birth blotches.

"You've gone quiet," he said. "I've offended you. I'm sorry."

For some reason that got me laughing.

"What's funny?" he asked, even though his voice hinted at laughing, too.

"My hand—you thought it was beautiful! And then you thought I'd be offended. . . ."

My heart is beautiful, Mama used to tell me, and my eyes, but never my blotchy face, never my browned and callused hands. If next to my own he'd seen my lady's pale, smooth hand. . . .

"Don't stop laughing!" he said, and he started to say things to get me to laugh again, telling a story of how he was once riding a horse that stopped suddenly, sending him flying off the saddle to land headfirst in a barrel of water. He wasn't satisfied that I was truly laughing then, so he sang the silliest song I guess I've ever heard. It was about a bodiless piglet, and I remember one verse of it because it repeated several times:

This morning I found a piglet,
  grunting beside my bed

This piglet, she had no body—
  she was only a head!
She rolled about while squealing,
  moving by snout and by jaw
Happily snuffling for treats
  without use of hoof or paw.

My lady even smiled, which made me feel fat with goodness. He did keep us laughing until fear of the guards was eating at him. Then he sent up a bag of fresh meat, raw and still warm.

"From an antelope my war chief slew for you. He's fierce with an arrow. I wish I could claim I'd slain it myself, but my clumsy shot went wide. I thought fresh meat might make a pleasant change."

"Oh, Khan Tegus, oh, my lord," I said, and that's all I could say for a few moments. "We have salt meat . . . but fresh, it's a difference, isn't it?"

"I'll say! Eating salt meat, you have to drink so much for your thirst, there's no room in the belly for food."

"And we have salted everything here—vegetables and meat and cheese and cracker bread. Though I'm not complaining, please don't think. The food's wonderful, as long as I can keep the rats out."

"There are rats?"

I hadn't meant to grumble, but there was this little pressure inside me, pushing inside my chest, urging me to confide some truth to him. "We've a plague of rats in the cellar. We swat at them and even got one in a trap, but I'm afraid my . . . my maid won't have enough to eat, after a time. My, uh, my father brought us so much food, but not enough for the rats, too."

"Your voice is tilting down, my lady," he said, "and I guess that you're frowning. You're worried. I should go now before the guards return, but keep the rats out of your hair tonight and I'll return tomorrow."

He left.

I don't have anything else to write, but I don't want to put down my brush yet. I want to keep all that happened, the feel of the evening still thick in my head, the sounds of his words awake in my ears, twitching pleasantly inside me. I'd guess I'm tower-addled and talking to someone from outside just made me wistful. That's all. That's why I feel this way, twisting and floating, as though my heart is bigger than my chest.

I do like the world quite a lot. Nothing more to say, so I'll draw.

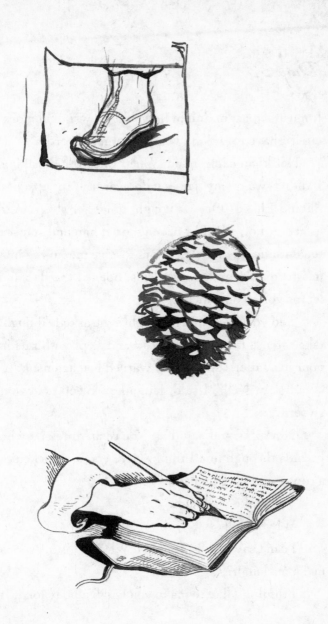

Day 33

It must be past midnight now, but I'll write till morning if I have to. I don't want to forget a word.

Her khan came again. When I heard him calling, I didn't wake my lady, who was asleep upstairs. Should I have? Or was it right to let her sleep? And asleep or not, should I have ignored him and refused to continue the lie? Ancestors forgive me, in the moment I didn't think twice. I just opened the flap and let his voice come in.

"Did you sleep well last night?" he asked. "I might take offense if you went ahead and slept with rats in your hair, after I specifically warned you against it."

"I slept well," I said, laughing. "Sleep is always sweet."

"Not all would say that. You're an antelope who bounds through life, I think. Here you are, locked in a tower and laughing still."

"You make me laugh."

"Why is that?"

"I can't say." And I couldn't. Why do his questions make me laugh?

"I think I'd like to make you laugh all day long. If

I could take you out of here, I'd hold a feast and a dance, and see you bedecked in a silver deel, laughing and bounding about."

"Why silver?"

"Because in the dark, your voice sounds silver."

My face burned feverish hot, so hot I thought I might die of the mud fever at once, but the feeling eased as I kept talking.

"That's a pretty thing to say." I forced my tone to sound light. "I wish I could think of pretty things to say, too, besides that your ankles are skinnier than a jackrabbit's ribs."

He cleared his throat. "It's just the cut of these boots, I assure you. And no excuses, my lady. You've had a flowery tongue in your time. Don't you remember our first letters?"

"It's been so long," I said, unhappy with the lie. "What did I say?"

Her khan chuckled. "Before coming here, I looked over all our letters, and the early ones, when you were thirteen and I fifteen. Well . . ."

"They were fairly ridiculous, weren't they?"

"In truth, you weren't so bad—more formal. You're very different to speak with in person. But I found some drafts of letters that I sent to you, and in one I wrote something akin to, 'When I think of you,

41

my heart melts like butter over the bread of my stomach.' I thought it was very poetic at the time. Or in another letter I wrote, 'You are like a shiny red apple with no worms.'"

I wanted to be respectful of his first words of love, but trying to hold in the laugh made me snort like a camel, and then he snorted, so laughs came rumbling out of me. We were trying not to laugh, of course—I didn't want to wake my lady and he didn't want to wake the guards, but that made it even harder to stop. How my side ached! I wheezed and said I couldn't breathe, which made him laugh harder, which in turn made me laugh harder because, truth be told, his laugh sounds like a yak's grunt. I told him as much, which was a mistake, because that brought up his laugh anew.

Can I describe what it felt like to sit in the dark, laughing with her khan through a bricked wall? The hard grayness lifted out of me like the bones from a fried fish. I felt strong enough to float, warmed as if by sunlight, my bones thrumming and my skin tingling. My mama used to say that the mightiest of the healing songs was a good laugh.

When we'd calmed down and I'd wiped the tears from my face, we sat in silence. I leaned against the wall, resting my head on the bricks. I could see by the angle of his boot that, outside, he was doing the same. It was almost like touching.

"My jaw hurts," I said.

"I can't stop grinning. Some of my warriors are watching for the guards a few paces off, and they're sure to think I've gone crazy."

"Maybe you have, did you think of that? You certainly sound crazy, laughing like a wild dog."

"Careful with the accusations of insanity, oh my lady whose home is a tower with windows of brick, all for the sake of some skinny-ankled, laugh-prone boy of a khan."

"If a lady is crazy to be bricked up in a tower, then what is a khan who sits outside to laugh with her?"

He sighed and groaned at once, the sound of his smile gone. "I'm sorry I can't break you out. I can't believe you don't despise me for it."

"Stop that. What's bothering you? I mean, besides this tower? I can hear your voice is tight, you've got an ache somewhere, nagging at you."

"How did you know? Yes . . . you're right. It's my leg. I was injured at sword practice last year. When I stand for a time . . ."

"My maid, she's a mucker girl, she knows the healing songs."

"The healing songs?"

"What a large world it is if there are people who never heard of the healing songs. Here, I'll have her sing to you. To work right, she should be touching your leg. Just you touch the leg yourself and listen, and close your eyes."

I crouched by the hole, down low so I was as close to him as I could be, and I sang the song for old injuries and wove it with the song for strong limbs, singing up with the coarse chanting of "High, high, a bird on a cloud," and singing down with the low swinging melody of "Tell her a secret that makes her sigh."

When I stopped, he was quiet for a good long moment. I could hear his breath, up and down like a bird's wings flapping.

"Thank you, my lady's maid," he said. "That was . . ."

He didn't finish, leaving me wondering. Some say hearing the songs makes them tickle inside, some say they feel as if they've suddenly gone hot to cold or cold to hot. Some say it's like dreaming while awake, or swimming while dry. I wish I knew how it felt inside her khan.

"My lady's maid, where did you learn such things?" he asked.

I gasped and bit my knuckle and wished I were

smarter than I am, but then I thought to say, "My maid is shy. She's a mucker and thinks she shouldn't speak to gentry, but she's grateful her song helped you."

"How does that work? I mean, the songs sing about birds and secrets and sighing, not about healing, nothing like the conjuring words of the shamans."

"What the words say doesn't matter. The sound of the words and the sound of the tune together speak a language that the body can understand . . . or so I've been told by my maid. The body wants to be whole, and when you sing the right sounds, you're reminding it how to heal itself."

"Can muckers heal? Does she have the power to stop blood flowing and stave off death?"

"Oh no, only the Ancestors have power of life. The healing songs just ease suffering, whether of body or mind. Times I've seen a man who'd decided to die, and a healing song changed his mind and let his body fight the disease off. I—my maid, she's never performed anything so grand. Though her mother has."

I could hear him move around, as if getting more comfortable, and lean his head closer to the hole.

"Keep talking, my lady. Your voice makes me want to stay and stay."

I lay down, resting my head on my hands, facing his voice. And I spoke. I wished I could whisper true things, about my mama, about the day my brothers left, about how a rainy spring makes the steppes grass so green you wish you were a yak so you could eat it. But I was being my lady, so I hid inside stories. I told the legend of how the Ancestors formed commoners from mud so there would be people in the world to serve their gentry children. He told me another that I'd never heard before, how Goda, goddess of sleep, took the form of a raven and first brought night to the world so all could rest. I would write down the exact tale here if I could recall it, but already some of his words slip away. All I remember for sure about that part of the conversation is I felt like I was riding a fast mare and I was sleeping in a warm blanket, both at the same time.

From outside, we heard a dog howl.

"That's a guard dog." His voice got a spice of anger in it. "Why do they have to come back so soon! Why don't they give us another hour of peace?"

I would've liked another hour myself.

"Listen," he said, "I am going to break you out. I'll come tomorrow night. I have enough warriors with me to kill the guards—"

"No, my lord, you can't just kill the guards!"

"Then we'll drug them somehow, and when they're sluggish and sleeping, we'll break down the—"

"No! Listen. My honored father is terribly mean,

he'll know it was you, he'll come after you. It'll be war between Titor's Garden and Song for Evela, sure enough. And if Lord Khasar hears you've taken us . . . he's a beast, I've heard. You don't want a war with him. We can wait for my . . . my father to soften. He's bound to let us out sometime, and meanwhile we're safe here." I believe that. Having now spent weeks in the darkness, I don't think her father will truly leave us here for seven years. No father could do that.

"But no, I . . ."

Her khan paused. He knew I was right. We couldn't start a war over a tower, not when my lady and I were alive and the cellar more full of food than of rats. The Ancestors bless him for hoping otherwise.

"It's all right, my lord. We'll be fine enough. We will."

"But my lady—"

"Just tell me, what's the sky look like tonight?"

Her khan sighed as if he were going to argue more, but then went quiet, and I imagined him looking up, squinting, waiting for the right words to fall into his head.

"The air is so clear, it shivers," he said. "All the stars are out, every one, even the babies. It's so bright with stars, the blacks of the sky look a dark, dark blue."

I could see it just like he said it.

"My lady." His voice was soft, as though there were no wall, as though he were right beside me. "I should return home. There's been unrest lately, Lord Khasar making threats and the like. I'll come again as soon as I can, and we'll see then if it's time to knock down this wall."

I said, "That's fine," though I didn't want him to leave. But I was speaking for my lady, and I spoke as I thought gentry would. "Your people should come first."

"I have a farewell gift," he said, a touch more brightness in his voice. "My chief of animals came on this journey, and she brought some companion animals along with the horses and yaks. When you mentioned your trouble with rats . . ."

I heard him call lightly to someone, then her khan's bare hand came through the hole, raising up something furry that mewed.

It was a yearling cat, long and lean, pale gray with green eyes. I put my face in its neck. It smelled of wind in the grass, of riverbed clay, of the world. I wanted to give him something in return, so I unhooked the neck clasp of my deel and shivered out of my shirt. It's just an undershirt, but it's what I wear closest to me and seemed the kind of a gift Lady Saren should offer her betrothed. Things worn closest to the skin, to the heart, carry the scent of a person, and of course, scent is the breath of the soul.

I leaned down, giving him the shirt. He took it, and took my hand, too. His hands were warm today, rough on the palms like well-used leather. And so much larger, my own hand nearly disappeared into his. He didn't say another word, but I felt different, as though he had sung to me the song for heartache, the one that goes, soft and slow, "Tilly tilly, nar a black bird, nilly nilly, there a blue bird."

Day 35

It's been two days since her khan left. We'll have the rest of his antelope meat tonight. I hope he has a safe journey.

I named the cat My Lord.

Day 39

I'm in love! My heart's so light it floats and carries me so my feet don't walk. I sing all day and I don't mind the washing, and that's how I know I'm in love. Completely smitten with My Lord the cat.

He's like a naked beech tree, sleek and gray. He's prettier than a morning sky and knows it, too. I shouldn't encourage him but I can't help it, and tell him all day long, "You're the prettiest cat in the world, My Lord, you're smarter than a dog and faster than a bird." I give him all the best bits from my dinner. Whenever I'm not singing to my lady's hidden ailment, I'm slathering the cat with songs.

My Lord has already killed three rats and I haven't heard so much as a good morning from the rest. And at night, do you know where he sleeps? With Dashti the mucker. The only cats I've known were so mangy their fur was half gone and they wheezed like startled snakes. But My Lord is gentry among beasts, a khan of cats.

And he always knows when it's day. Times there are when I wake thinking that it's morning, only to peer out the flap and see darkness thick as stew. Time makes no sense in a dark prison. But My Lord the cat knows the time. As soon as it's morning, he stands on my chest, touches his cold nose to mine, and breathes on my lips.

I'd ask my lady if she'd prefer My Lord to sleep with her, but Titor, god of animals, himself can't force a cat to change his mind. Besides, it might not be proper to share a bed with a cat, she being an honored lady and all.

Day 48

Two weeks since her khan left. I asked my lady how far to his home in Song for Evela, and she thinks it'd take about two weeks, so perhaps he's already home.

Today I find myself remembering one night as a little girl, when our gher was still full of family, and a traveling shaman stayed the night. It's good luck to offer any stranger one night under your felt roof, but doubly so for a shaman. How excited we were! I remember watching the shaman with wide eyes and doing my best to blink as little as possible. If he turned into a fox, as I'd always heard shamans can, I was determined not to miss the sight. The shaman didn't transform that night, but he told us stories of the Ancestors and what they willed us to do in order to enter their Realm one day. And he told us how gentry were the children of the Ancestors, how it was a commoner's privilege to serve them. It was the first I'd ever heard of gentry.

Many times after that night I liked to lie back and imagine what the gentry might be like—skin that glows like a candle, eyes shining with the wisdom of the Ancestors. Sometimes I actually thought they might have tails like foxes or butterfly wings. Then meeting Lady Saren and her father . . .

But now I've spoken with Khan Tegus, and though his hand didn't glow or anything, there was something in his voice, in his words, that was different than anyone I've ever known. The mark of the Ancestors must be in him, stronger than in some gentry. Maybe that's why his title is khan instead of just lord. I'll ask my lady.

Lady Saren told me a story tonight while she petted My Lord the cat. How many things she must know!

She said that the Eight Realms were once united under a Great Khan, and the seat of his power was Song for Evela. Now all the realms have their own lord or lady rulers, but in memory of the Great Khan, the ruler of Song for Evela still carries the title of khan. I asked her how she knew, and she said all gentry families keep the history of wars and marriages and so on. Such a thing as history never occurred to me before.

Day 73

It's fully winter now. There's a rim of ice on our well that I have to crack with the bucket. Each time I open the metal flap to the outside, I get blasted by cold. The wash water freezes as I pour it on the ground, and afterward I spend several minutes before the fire just to get color back in my hands. This time of year, it's too cold to snow. High winter out-of-doors is death as sure as a knife in the chest, and a winter's funeral brings bad luck to the whole clan.

I'm a mucker, so I thought I knew winter, but from inside this tower I've learned something new—the winter wind has its own voice. Autumn wind has a gusty warmth to it and a lower tone as though it sings from deep in the belly. The winter wind screeches around the tower, singing the high harmony, its voice sharp with ice. My lady isn't fond of that sound.

A few days ago, I carried her mattress down to the main floor and shut the door in the ceiling so we keep in more of the fire's heat. I think even the Ancestors understand that in winter, a mucker maid and a lady must sleep side by side.

Surely her khan won't return until after winter. Spring seems as far off as the Ancestors' Realm.

Day 92

Yesterday smoke was filling our room something awful, and in a locked tower, air filled with smoke would kill us right quick. I rolled up my lady in all our blankets before I smothered our fire. In the time it took me to clean out the blocked chimney, my jaw was hammering and my fingertips turned blue. I relit the fire and shivered on my mattress until the room warmed again, there being not a spare blanket for my shoulders.

This winter, Goda, goddess of sleep, must have made Evela, goddess of sunlight, awfully drowsy. No memory of sunshine hangs in the air. Everything feels gray and hard and dark. I guess that might make me bitterly sad, but right now, My Lord is asleep on my lap.

Day 98

The guards only bring our daily milk every two days now, sometimes three. In the cold, they must stay in their tents, keeping the fire going nice and toasty, venturing out only to milk their animals and make yellow ice.

To help our milk last three days, I add water. It wouldn't be proper for my lady to drink plain water, as if she were poorer than poor. Even Mama and I always had milk to drink.

Day 122

Little to record. I wash, I cook. I stoke the fire. Whenever the wind moans, my lady shivers as though she feels it on her skin. She's refused to bathe for weeks, but this morning I insisted. When I dunked her hair into a bucket of water, there was a powerful scent, reminding me of the time my brothers' reindeer fell into a stream.

Today, for the first time, I couldn't enjoy the spices in the food. It was as though I couldn't taste them. I can't say why that was.

Still, My Lord the cat is so beautiful.

Day 141

The middle night. I just woke after a dream, though it was the kind of dream that's more memory than imagination. I saw again the last night her khan was here, the sight of his hand lifting up the cat. And then I saw what I gave him in return. I hadn't thought of it again since that night. The memory jolted me awake.

I gave her khan my shirt. Ancestors, there was a basket of washing right by my mattress. I could've seized one of my lady's own shirts. He would've inhaled her scent, the breath of *her* soul. Even though there was something else at hand, I chose to give him my own garment.

Why didn't the Ancestors strike me dead? After such an offense, I'd think they wouldn't permit this mucker maid to remain breathing. Perhaps they only ignore me because I'm shut up in this tower, cut off from the gaze of the Eternal Blue Sky. Perhaps if

I ever step out of its shadow, I'll be struck in the instant and crumble into a heap of ash.

Day 158

This morning, we . . . I'm shaking still. I didn't realize until I put the brush to paper. If My Lord the cat weren't on my lap, I don't know that I could be calm enough to write at all.

This morning, we heard voices outside. Now that it's warm enough for the sun to burn holes in the icy ground, we've begun to hear our guards again, chatting as they walk around the tower and occasionally shouting saucy things at us. But these voices were new. One was so deep and loud, I felt it in the stones of the tower. I felt it in my bones.

I was darning my lady's stockings by the orange light of the fire, and my lady was lying on my bed, teasing My Lord the cat with a stocking too holey to save. When we heard the new voices, she sat upright, like a fawn stops grazing when she hears a hunter's step.

"Is it your khan, do you think?" I asked. "Back already?"

My lady didn't answer. She's so often spooked,

I didn't realize that this time she was truly terrified, so badly that she couldn't speak or move.

I left my sewing, fetched the wooden spoon, unhooked the flap, and jammed it open.

"Don't, Dashti," she said too late, just as a hand shot up the hole and seized my arm.

I screamed, I think. The hand was covered in a black gauntlet, the wrist trimmed in metal spikes. It was not her khan.

"Do I have her?" said the voice low enough to grumble in stones. "Do I have my lady?"

"No, I'm sorry, no, no," I said.

"Who is this?" He shook my arm.

"I'm Dashti. I'm my lady's maid. I'm the mucker maid."

He laughed as if I'd just told a wicked joke. "Yes, I know muckers. There are hundreds of the ragged folk wandering the steppes in Thoughts of Under."

He let go, and I pulled my arm inside.

"Put your arm back!" He yelled so loud, the cat screeched.

I didn't want to. Ancestors, I wanted to crawl under my mattress. He may have a voice like an earth rumble and put my lady in the fear shakes, but I recognized the command of gentry, and I must do what he says. I lowered my arm back down the hole.

He didn't grab me again, just tickled his gloved fingers against my fingertips. He was chuckling, lower than his voice. Then he slapped my hand against the wall. It stung like a log full of hornets.

I pulled my arm up, but he said, really slowly and sweetly like I was his favorite lamb, "Back down, Dashti the mucker maid."

Again I lowered my hand, and again he slapped it against the wall. I left it there, and I was crying, but not just because it hurt, I think. The next time he slapped, my lady grabbed me under the arms and pulled me away from the hole. We fell back on my mattress.

"Stay here," she said.

I stayed. After all, she's my own mistress. Let that black-gloved lord growl and yell all he likes, I'll obey her first.

"It's him. It's Lord Khasar," said my lady.

And I stopped wondering why she refused to marry him.

"Are you in there, Lady Saren? Do you believe you're hiding, stashed in a tower all the world can see? You're not very good at the hiding game. You never were."

I wish I could write that my lady stood tall, that she declared she would never love him or bow to him or tremble at his voice, let him do his worst, or somewhat of that bold kind of talking. I saw her show a bit of courage to her father once, but at Lord Khasar's voice, she covered her face and cried so hard she squeaked like rusted hinges. I'm sorry for her, I am, but sometimes I think crying's done for and it's time for doing. If only I knew what ailed her, perhaps I could help, but I guess there are corners and folds of my lady's soul that I'll never see.

I sat with her, put one hand on her belly and one on her back, and sang the song for bitter sorrow, the one that goes, "Darker river, blacker river, faster river, pulling me." I sang while Lord Khasar spoke. She calmed some. I didn't dare go pull the wooden spoon and shut the flap. He couldn't touch us, safe here in the center of the room, but his voice slinked in like smoke. Not even in the cellar under sacks of barley would we be able to hide from that sound.

These are the sorts of things he said.

"Your father hobbled to Thoughts of Under to see me, whining like a girl in two braids. He told me, 'My daughter awaits you in the watchtower on the border of our lands. Knock down the walls! Take her, bound and gagged, I care not. She is refuse to me till she bends her will to your own.' He spoke grandly, but his knees shook. Do your knees shake, my lady? I don't trust a man who fears me, and all fear me.

Do you fear me, my lady?" He laughed heartily at that.

"I remember your eyes when we first met. You were eleven years old? Twelve? Your eyes were as dull as a cow's, but you looked lovely dressed in silks. You still do, don't you, my jewel? You are beautiful adorned in gold, so who cares about your dim eyes?

"And I remember how your eyes changed after sleeping one night in my house. You no longer had cow eyes, but mouse eyes, rabbit eyes, the wide eyes of prey. How much I enjoyed that night, I really can't express. Besides you, there's only one other person still living whom I've allowed to see me feeding. I hope you feel that honor, Lady Saren. I trusted you with that secret because I know you'd never dare tell."

Here he laughed with a dark, dry rasp, and I wished I knew what he was speaking about. My lady lay on my bed, one arm wrapped around her face, the other clinging to my waist, her entire body quaking.

"That's when I wanted you as my own. I told your father then that you would be my bride. But I won't knock down this tower for you, not today. I won't force you out yet. I'm having too much fun."

His voice was nearly a whisper, and yet we could still hear. "The day will come when you will choose me over the tower. Knowing what you know, you will still choose me. I hunger for that day."

Then for some time, silence.

I think he'd been gone a long while by the time we could sit up and breathe. My lady still clung to me. I was too shaken to sing anymore, my voice felt sticky and my heart clattered about, so I held her till she could stop shaking, too.

"You'd met him before, my lady? You knew his temperament, that's why you refused to wed."

"Yes," she said. There were secrets laden in that word "yes" that she didn't explain. I could feel it, and it made me afraid.

"His voice is heavier than lead," I said. "And he slaps harder than your honored father. Do all gentry slap people? I suppose it's a noble's right, but I wonder, your khan doesn't seem like to slap."

"No," she said. "I chose him because I thought he was safe."

She was so beautiful as she said those words, even with the red eyes of crying. She made me believe she could choose whomever she wanted, and the poor man would have no choice but to fall in love with her, too. Perhaps even Lord Khasar was in love with her, in his own way.

"Did Khan Tegus make you laugh?" I asked.

She shrugged, and I realized I'd never heard her laugh. She pulled her knees up and stared at the fabric of her deel stretched tight between them. She took a deep breath and I hoped, hoped, hoped it meant that she was going to talk more. It's so rare with my lady. I don't know if she was always a quiet one or if her will to speak has been smothered by the tower darkness. When she opened her mouth, I had to suppress a sigh of contentment.

"After my father and I spent time at Lord Khasar's house, after I saw what that man was, I thought to betroth myself to someone else before Khasar officially asked. I knew he would ask, as soon as I turned sixteen and was of an age. I chose Khan Tegus. He was on friendly terms with my father and I thought him gentler than most. We wrote letters for years. I told my maid Qara what to say and she wrote for me. Qara was my best friend. When my father condemned me to this tower, she ran away."

My lady's eyes were empty as she spoke. I shivered, imagining being a child in that large house with floor stones that look to be cut from ice instead of passing winter nights in a snug gher. To be raised by a fierce lord who slaps instead of by a mama who sings.

This was the most my lady had ever confided in me, and I longed to keep her talking. "How did you first know you loved Khan Tegus? Did you—"

"I'm tired," she said and climbed the ladder to bed.

And that's how it is with my lady. Sometimes we share a few words about the food or My Lord's prowess with the rats or the cold that burrows between bricks, but let me broach the topic of her khan, or black-gloved Lord Khasar, or her father and his house, and my lady is suddenly as tired as a weeping willow in full leaf.

My Lord the cat is asleep on me or I would've ended my account and gone to bed long ago. His purring shakes my lap but steadies my hand.

Day 160

The guards generally don't speak with us. Sometimes they shout at us, but they don't expect a response. Times I've asked them for news of the world, for fresh meat, for anything. Even knowing they'll say no, it's a thrill to holler through the hole and know that another person hears my voice and might answer. Her honored father must have warned them sharply to leave us well alone, but this morning I got one to speak.

I held open the flap to dump the wash water and splashed someone's boots.

"Watch it, now!"

"Sorry," I said, not afraid, for I knew the voice as belonging to one of our regular guards. "Is he gone?"

"Lord Khasar? Yes, gone two nights ago, thank the Ancestors."

"Did he hurt any of you?" My hand still smarted from the bashing and made scrubbing my lady's stockings and unders no pleasant task.

"Not much," he said.

It was more than he'd spoken to me in all our tower days, so I risked more questions.

"Can you tell me, what does the sky look like today?"

"Sky? It looks like a sky."

"Is it blue?"

The guard snorted. "It's always blue."

But he's wrong. Though we call it the Eternal Blue Sky, I know that sometimes it's black, sometimes white, sometimes yellow, pink, purple, gray, black, peach, gold, orange, a dozen different shades of blue with a hundred different kinds of clouds in thousands of shapes. That's what makes it so wondrous. If the guard couldn't see that, I wouldn't bother to explain.

"What of the world?" I asked. "Is there news from Titor's Garden? From my lady's family?"

The guard laughed like a horse snorts. "I feel like I'm talking to the dead. You're not coming out of that tower, miss, not unless that lord from Thoughts of Under breaks you out, and then he'd snap a maid's neck and toss her to the dogs, more than like. Enjoy your brick room and don't worry about what's outside. Nothing here belongs to you anymore."

He was laughing when he said it, but I could read his voice plain as my own letters—he was sorry for us, and he was sorry for being sorry.

They weren't nice words he said. He could've lived a good life and died never having made a person feel rubbed down to bones and too sad to hold together. Still, it can't be an easy thing, guarding two girls who've been thrown into the rubbish heap of Under, god of tricks. I think he laughs because he doesn't want to hurt for us.

While he was still close enough to hear, I sang the song for stone hearts, the one with the bristling tune that goes, "Chick tight in a shell, wings up and away." He listened some, then walked on.

Day 162

Spring's here, the first breath of it anyway. The stone floor is not so cold at night, and the air coming in from outside, which used to smell like a hole dug deep, now smells like blue sky. My Lord senses the change, too. He's friskier, wants to jump and play, and I exercise him with stockings and bits of salt meat.

I thought my lady's mood might change with the season, but she's still the same, her back rounded more than straight, her eyes dim. I try new songs on her, I combine songs. Though sometimes her temper lifts, the change never lasts long. But I'm mucker stubborn, and I'm determined to discover her ailment.

A fresh breeze just found its way up the dump hole. I wish I could see the buds on the trees, just trembling to open and be leaves, and hear all the honeybees out and buzzing, so happy to be free of their winter hideaway they're like to burst.

Day 180

I would write more if I had something to say. I'll draw here the profile of my lady as she stares at the wall. She's been sitting in silence since dinner, and it's nearly time for supper.

Day 223

This past week I was wishing for something new to happen so I could have a reason to write. It's bad luck to make a vague wish like that, because Under, god of tricks, is bound to grant it with something unpleasant. And so he did.

Lord Khasar returned today.

"I'm back, my lady, my love!" He shouted heartily, as though he called all the world to dinner.

"I wish I could hit him," said my lady. "When I think of him, I want to punch him with all my strength. I wouldn't care if he hit me back, if only I could hit him once, hard, between the eyes."

That sounded like a very nice plan to me.

There was a knock on the flap, and we took a step back.

"Go away," I said. "My lady doesn't want you. Leave us be!"

There was some clanking and scraping, the noises seeming to come from all around us. We stood in the center of the room, I holding my lady's hands. Then with a shriek of metal, the flap tore right out of the bricks. My lady screamed and jumped back against the far wall.

"If you don't open up when I knock, I'll have to tear down the door," said Lord Khasar. His voice echoed up in our tower, loud as thoughts. "Come give me your hand, mucker maid."

"Stay, Dashti," said my lady, the Ancestors bless her.

Lord Khasar laughed in his way, low and loud. "Is it time to come home yet, Lady Saren? Are you well pickled in this barrel? Shall I break you out?"

"Tell him no," I whispered. My lady wouldn't speak.

"Nothing to say? Then perhaps I should burn you out," he said.

Something flicked up the hole. I didn't see where it landed till the smoke started. My mattress was on fire. I leaped at it, stomping on the burning straw. Then another fiery chip shot into the room, and another. More and more rained down with near-silent ticks. Some fizzled on dry stone, but others found cloth, wood, and straw, and set in to smoke or burn. My lady ran with me, stamping at anything bright. If fire took hold, we'd cook in this stove of a tower long before a wall could be knocked down.

All I could think was out, out, out, as I ran and stomped and slapped. My lady began to scream hysterics and pound at the bricks, and I was left to fight the little fires alone. My breath was scraping hard in my throat and the smoke made me want to vomit.

"Behind you!" she shouted, pointing. A washcloth was burning hard right by the stack of wood, and if the wood caught fire, we'd be rabbits in the pot, no question. I flung myself at the rag, rolling over it to squash the flames.

I was aching and sweating when the fire chips stopped coming. My lady collapsed on my partly charred mattress, her eyes staring at the ceiling. I don't know if we'd fought the smoke and flames for minutes or hours, but I guess I never felt so scared in all my life.

"I wish I could have witnessed that dance!" said Lord Khasar. What a horrid sound his voice is, how greasy black his every word. "But you will dance for me yet, my willow flower. Will it be tonight? Tell me now, Lady Saren, because I won't come again until your seven years are over. Will you choose six more years in this dungeon or the rest of your life in my house? My house where you will have ten lady's maids and ten times that many deels, fresh food, warm baths, a large room with five windows and a door to the garden. A garden, my lady, rimmed with flowers in the summer that will bow to your beauty. And the only cost is," here his voice went very dry, "you will share that house with me."

His voice had become both softer and louder. I guessed his face was right up under the hole where the flap used to be.

My lady's chamber pot stood by my feet, waiting for disposal. Well, my lady stood up, tore off the cover, and dumped it down the hole with a slosh and a splash. All her waste, both the liquid and the muddy kind, must've spilled onto his face, right into his open, shouting mouth.

He hollered, and rightly so. We held so still it hurt, but we haven't heard Lord Khasar's voice since. Never have I felt prouder to be maid to Lady Saren.

After a few moments, I giggled. My lady giggled. Then we lay back together and laughed in a tight way, as though we actually cried.

Later

There's howling outside.

My lady is curled up in the center of the room. She won't speak to me. I lay beside her and sang the lulling song for comfort, the one that goes, "Trails of poppy, poppy, poppy," but a song of healing can't help if the person won't will it. Right now, I guess, she needs to be terrified. I don't want to be. I hoped writing would help.

There's another howl. Why does that sound dance like fingernails down my back? I've heard wolves call out before. When my family kept sheep, a howl was a useful noise, a reminder to gather in any of the herd we didn't want to lose that night. And if a wolf got too near, my brothers would sing the song of the wolf, a baying tune that made the wolves want to howl back but also invited them to leave us be. And they always did. There are far worse things than wolves.

My Lord the cat is sitting on my lap. The hair on his neck is up straight as trees, and he mews hard at each howl. The sound is getting closer. With the metal flap torn off, I can see it is black night outside. I should put some kind of cover there, but I don't dare get closer.

Something's happening. There's no more howl-ing, only snarls. The guards' dogs were barking fit to burst, but now they've gone quiet. I hear our guards shouting one at another, I hear one of them scream. There's another. Ancestors, there's another scream. What's happening? It doesn't sound like battle. It sounds like nightmares.

My lady still trembles. My Lord the cat is hiss-ing. I stroke him and sing. I wish someone would sing to me. There's a scream again, just outside the —

I write from awful silence now. I was interrupted before by a cry for help, so close, right at the mouth of the hole, so I crept closer to see if I could give aid.

Of a sudden, the jaws of a wild animal shot up, growling and snapping at me. A wolf, I think, but enormous, and its mouth was smeared with blood. Did it come from the woods? Or is it possible Lord Khasar breeds wolves to be blood hungry for battle?

I fell back on the floor and tried to scoot away. It couldn't get in, it was much too large, but its mouth drooled and snapped at me, the nose sniffed the air as if hunting.

Then, too late, I saw My Lord crouched, preparing to pounce.

"No!" I shouted and leaped forward, trying to hold him back, but I missed. My Lord jumped at the thing, snarling and shrieking. Both animals disappeared down the hole. I heard horrible growls from the beast, and a yelp from the cat. But not a cry of pain, I think. I hope. Oh, my cat, my sleek gray cat.

All was quiet again. My lady didn't weep, she just stayed in her ball, shaking. I ran back and forth, trying to comfort my lady and returning to look for My Lord at the hole. Nothing in the world seemed alive but me, and I didn't much want to be.

Many aching minutes later, I dared to get close to the hole. I feared those snapping wolf jaws or that black-gloved hand, but I placed myself near enough to call out.

"Is anyone there? Hello? Please answer."

I heard nothing from the guards. They don't always answer, perhaps they ran off or are hiding. Perhaps.

Please, Titor, god of animals, please keep My Lord the cat. Please keep him safe.

Day 224

No sign of My Lord the cat. No sound from the guards.

Day 225

My Lord hasn't returned. I wait by the hole and I call. Still no sound from our guards.

Day 231

My Lord the cat used to make a little hiccup sound in his throat whenever he jumped onto the table. His favorite treat was cheese. When he attacked a rat, he was deadly fast, going straight for a fatal bite on the back of the neck. When he ate the rat, he was meticulous, finding his favorite bits first, spending hours to consume the whole. When he was deep asleep, he sometimes meowed, a sound of total contentment. I didn't mind waking up to that noise, not a bit.

Day 236

My lady says My Lord is gone, killed by Khasar.

"Why would Lord Khasar kill a cat?" I asked.

"I know things," she said. "People think I'm not smart, but some things I know."

She wouldn't tell me what she knows. Sometimes I feel lonely with her sitting right beside me.

And where are the guards? They haven't brought milk since Khasar was here. Maybe they're all right and just ran home to the city to report to my lady's father. I hope they come back soon. Without fresh milk, I've had to mix dried yogurt into my lady's water. It's clumpy and tastes sour, but at least she won't have to drink plain water.

And worse news—the rats are back. Just a few days without a cat and already they return. I hear them scratching and yipping and rustling down there. I set up more traps, but they avoid them. The washing isn't done and we had a cold lunch because I stay hours in the cellar, trying to smack rats with a broom.

I think My Lord the cat must be fine. He'll come back soon.

Day 240

My lady offered to sit a spell down below combating rats so I could warm my hands and make dinner. It seemed a task not fit for gentry, and when I protested, she insisted she'd do it. I supposed if she was willing, then it would be all right.

When the meal was laid out on our little table, I called her up from the cellar. My lady climbed the ladder and made straight for the upper chamber.

"I don't feel well," she said. "I'm going to bed early."

"Let me come sing to you," I offered. But she refused.

When I returned to the cellar for more rat swatting, I found the culprit of her illness — my lady had eaten half a bag of sugar.

Day 245

Every day, my lady says she will take a turn whacking rats, but really she's down there eating. Rats squeal and skitter around her, and I hear her lips smack, smack, smack.

Day 268

She's devoured our dried fruit, every crumb, and all the sugar's gone but dust. Now she's demanding I soak more meat overnight, cook larger meals and more bread. I tried to argue once, but she raised her hand and commanded me to obey on the sacred nine. So I do. Though I grumble enough to put any piglet to shame.

Six more years, and not a grain of sugar. Six more years and no fruit, fresh or dry.

Later

It appears she also ate the last wheel of cheese. The rats will be heartbroken.

Day 281

Last night or morning or whatever time it was, I sat by the fire taking out the seams in my lady's clothing and stitching them back up broad. Since she's taken to eating, she's rounder than before.

I told her, "My lady, our food supply's in peril. We have to be careful."

"It doesn't matter," she said. "We won't last seven years anyway."

That made us both quiet. She stared at the fire for so long, I wondered what thoughts rode the flames in her vision. Then she asked me, "Dashti, would you have married Lord Khasar?"

"No! I'm a mucker, I couldn't marry a member of the gentry."

"But imagine if you were me, would you?"

I tried to imagine. Even how he slaps hands and flicks burning chips into our tower, even though his voice makes my stomach spin, would I marry him to escape this coffin? After falling in love with her khan, would the thought of being with any other man make me weep and tangle my hair? Would I have chosen to lock myself up for seven years and even die from darkness? I tried to imagine, but it made me dizzy, and I couldn't keep my eyes on the stitching. *Stop*. Just thinking of a commoner marrying gentry is a gross sin of the kind that could get me noosed on the city's south wall and never welcomed into the eternal Realm of the Ancestors. She's wrong to make me think it.

My only reply was, "You do what you think's best, my lady. If you'd rather wed Lord Khasar than be in this tower another day, I'll stay with you all the same."

I didn't want to say that, but I did, and I meant it. I'm her lady's maid, I swore an oath, and I'll serve her till I die.

She smiled, and I saw her cheeks dimple for the first time since we met. What a sad little bird she usually is, how she droops and moans when she could be as brilliant as the sun. Sometimes I forget that she's gentry, that her blood is divine. But when she smiled, I remembered—she is as beautiful as light on water.

She looked back at the fire. "I know I should have married Lord Khasar. I was born to marry. That's my only purpose."

"That can't be, my lady."

"My father told me so when I was small enough to sit on his knee. My older sister, Altan, she'll be the lady of the realm after my father. I have an older brother, Erdene, who will rule if Altan were to die. I'm the third child. I used to dream I'd be chief of animals one day. I like animals. But my father said I'm too dull-witted. And besides, I'm gentry—any commoner can be raised up to be a chief. But the third child of a ruling lord is only fit for marrying off to other gentry."

I could tell by the way my lady stared at the fire that

she was done talking, so I sat by her, quiet, and thought about what she'd said. Her sister's name, Altan, means *golden* in the naming language. Gold is the color of the gentry, and it seems a right name for the lady of a realm. Erdene means *jewel*, another noble name. Saren means *moonlight*. I wonder what her mother thought when she named her moonlight, the dim light that keeps the night sky company until the blue sky can return.

It's strange for me to think about gentry in that way, as people who had mothers who gave them names. People who wanted things they couldn't have, who were ordered to marry men they feared. Though I clean her plate and wash her unders, I guess until today, I never truly thought of my lady as a real person.

Later

I showed my lady the drawing I did of her smiling, and she said that I'm her best friend. I thought I should write that down.

Day 298

Daily I sing to my lady. Sometimes it's to help ease a headache or bellyache, and sometimes it's my continued attempt to cure whatever troubles her inside. Yesterday I tried a new song, one I'd nearly forgotten.

The song for unknown ailments is a wail. High the notes stretch, my throat stretching with them, the tune reaching up and up like a wounded bird's call, "Rain rips as it falls, it tears as it falls!" Just the sound of it echoing in our tower made my chest feel tight. My lady sighed and curled up against me, not crying but breathing as if she would. After she had a good rest, she seemed lighter. She even chatted with me over supper and joined me in a game of pea toss.

So I went to bed content last night, thinking I'd made some progress with her healing. But this morning she's the same again. If only she'd tell me why she's so sad and crooked-brained and lonely and often acts as if she's only half her age. Does *she* even know why? Maybe it's just how she is, maybe there's nothing in her to fix.

I'll keep trying.

Day 312

It's summer, and thank Evela, goddess of sunlight, that it's a gentle one this year or we'd roast in our brick oven. There were children running around our tower this morning. I think they've been here before, but I could hear them more clearly today. They were closer to the tower, perhaps daring one another to draw near, and their voices ghosted up the uncovered hole. As they ran around and around, I could hear broken bits of the song they sang. I believe it went like this:

Two dead ladies in a tower
Counting peas for every hour
In seven years

With all their tears
They drown in pea soup sour

I didn't care for their song much, but I sat near the hole all the same and listened, listened, listened. New sounds are like lost sugar.

Day 339

Most of the time, my lady sits alone and stares at things—her fingers, the floor, a single hair. I wonder how a person can sit so much without work in her hands. Are muckers born to work and gentry born to sit? This darkness makes me ask questions that never occurred to me under the Eternal Blue Sky.

But it doesn't seem fair, does it? Why can't my lady dip her hands into the wash water and give the clothes a good scrubbing or mend a rip or make a pot of something worth eating? I'd be pleased as anything if I never had to haul a bucket of water up the cellar ladder again, but some work isn't so bad, not when you have naught else to do but stare at a candle flame or into the shivering dark.

Later

Ancestors forgive me, but I offered to teach my lady how to cook dung cakes.

She said, "I don't know how, Dashti."

"That's why I'll teach you."

"I'll do it wrong."

"Of course you will, everyone does wrong when learning something new."

Then she started to cry. "But I'll do it *wrong*."

I wish I understood my lady and her crying and her shaking. She looks at the whole world as though it crouches over, ready to pounce.

Day 457

Weeks and weeks go by, months and months. I wash, I cook. My lady is more shadow than girl. Once I tried to teach her to read. Her eyes wandered.

Some days I hate candlelight. Sometimes I think we'd be better in all darkness, then we'd just hold still until everything went away. But I keep cooking.

I keep washing. I keep singing. And I keep the fire and candles lit.

Day 528

Today I thought I would like to die, so I went into the cellar and smacked a few rats with the broom. It helped some.

Day 640

This summer is worse than last. The heat, heat, heat pushes against the walls of the tower, forces its way inside, and yells silently in our faces. We sit in the cellar, underground where it's a little cooler, and keep the rats company. Or we sit upstairs, where the barest slip of breeze comes through the crack between bricks. I can't light fires, lest we die of the heat. We eat cold food. We pour water over our heads and shiver.

The hearth is left bare for summer, and I feel as though we're living with eyes shut. Day and night we keep a candle burning, and that tiny fingertip of light wobbles before me, as if too weak to live on, gasping its last breath. It creates more shadows than light, filling the tower with corners. When my lady sits against a far wall, she disappears.

I don't dare light more than one candle. The rats have eaten many. A dying wasp of candlelight is so much better than none.

Some days I look at the bricks in the door and wonder how hard I'd have to hit them to knock one loose. If I managed to break us out, would the guards shoot me with their arrows? Are they even there anymore? Would her honored father know of our escape and stuff us back in for another seven years? Would Lord Khasar hunt us down?

This is more thinking than I've done in months, and I'm tired now. The heat is so huge, I have no space left for thoughts.

Day 684

Here's something true about darkness—after enough time, you begin to see things that aren't there. Faces look at me, and when I turn my head, they disappear. Colors wash themselves before my eyes, then fade away. Shiny gray dream rats dart between my feet but don't make a sound. I wanted to write this down so I can remember that those things aren't real.

My lady sees more than I do. Sometimes what she sees makes her cry.

Day 723

I think my . . . I think I . . .

What was I going to write? I can't think of words. The candle flame is glaring at me. My lady moans. I'm going to go to bed now.

Day 780

It's winter again. Over two years behind bricks. For weeks and weeks, my brain felt slow as ice pouring, but the past days, thoughts and questions and memories have started to roil in my head again. Is it a sign that something's going to happen soon? The longer I'm in the dark, the more memories are brighter in my eyes than the bricks in the wall. I begin to feel surrounded by ghosts, people long gone pressing around me.

My father died before I was old enough to call him Papa. It should've been all right for us because

Mama had three sons before me. The oldest was fourteen, of an age to hunt for food and protect us, as sons are supposed to do. And he did, for five years. But then we had a standing-death winter, when the night gets cold sudden fast, the air freezes like ice, and in the morning you find the horses and yaks and sheep dead on their feet.

Our family hadn't belonged to a clan for years, so we were on our own.

Three days after the animals died, my mama and I woke to discover my brothers gone. Their boots gone. Their bedrolls and knives and belts. Gone. I understand why they left us. With a mother and a young girl, they'd have little chance to earn enough to trade for new animals. Alone, they could pledge themselves to another clan, work for seven years, then find a bride in that clan and build up their own herd. But with father and animals dead, our family was a grave.

Mama and I were hungry lots after that, but we had our gher and one animal left, a mare named Weedflower who still gave milk.

We didn't dare go to the main pasturing places. Any mucker out of luck would see a woman and a girl with no men to protect them as an invitation to plunder. And besides, with only one animal, we couldn't live the life of a herder. So we camped near forests where we could hunt for small animals and gather what the trees would give us. We hunched up in the coldest places, the driest, the least inviting, where no one else wanted to be. And times when we had to go near the city to do piecework to trade for cloth or tools, we smeared Weedflower's dung in our hair and wore our rags, so no man would be tempted to carry one of us off.

We survived. And with Mama's singing, we stayed healthy enough. We may've eaten mudfish more than rabbit and stick birds more than antelope, we may've watered the milk gray and slept with our mare inside the gher for warmth, but times there were when we laughed enough to shake the forest and ripple the rivers. Times I thought, good riddance to my brothers. They don't know what they missed.

Here's a memory of my mama and home that my fingers long to draw:

And then I get to remembering when she died. I was fourteen. I'd been crying too much and was weak as wet laundry. But I laid her out on the open steppes under the Eternal Blue Sky, with her feet pointed at the Sacred Mountain so her soul would know which way to walk. I sat with her another day and night. I told her stories about our life together so her soul could remember who she was, then I sang her the parting songs. The songs that tell her spirit that she's ready to go, that it's all right, that she can leave me now and walk up the Sacred Mountain and back down again into the Ancestors' Realm. In cities, singing the soul out of the body is a shaman's work, but we muckers had to learn those songs ourselves, with no shaman around for miles.

I guess singing the parting songs to my mama was the hardest thing I've ever done. I would've rather had her ghost haunting my every footstep than be alone. But I felt proud after I did it. And now she'll be waiting in the Ancestors' Realm, ready to sing me in.

We were camped a long way from the city that summer, so far it made my legs hurt just to think of the distance. I took apart the gher and loaded as much as I could on Weedflower's back and the rest on my own. I had to leave the gher's heavy winter coverings behind, cast off to rot on the ground. It wasn't easy to do. Mama and I had pressed the wool ourselves to make the felt—aching work, longtime work. But what could I do? The load was already heavy enough to make me stagger.

As I walked toward the summer pastures, I offered Weedflower as a gift to everyone I met. None robbed me, thank the Ancestors, but none accepted my gift. If they had, it'd be the same as consenting to make me a member of their family and agreeing to one day find me a husband. It'd been a hard winter. None wanted another mouth to feed. Maybe if I were prettier. Maybe if I didn't have the red blotches on my face and arm, the sign of an ill-fated life.

I always thought I'd be a mucker bride, become a mama like my own one day. It's only now, as my brush touches this page, that I'm realizing I never will. I wish My Lord the cat were curled up in my lap and purring.

Eventually I found a clan headed toward the city, and I exchanged my gher for a place in their Long Walk. It was summer, so I could sleep on the ground. I had Weedflower's milk to drink, and I hunted for roots and birds and rodents when I could, and traded milk for a bowl of food from other people's pots. I'd never been around so many folk before, and yet it was the loneliest I ever felt. Is that strange? Well, the loneliest except for now in this tower.

I miss Weedflower, whom I had to sell in order to buy myself employment and lodging at the house of chiefs. I miss myself, how I used to be. How I used to feel under the sky. I miss the time when I could believe I'd die old with my own husband beside me, one who wouldn't think of me as a mouth to feed or leave after a standing-death winter.

I just looked at the dump hole and saw light outside. Morning? Did I write all night? Time is a wind that keeps blowing in my face and mumbling words that don't make sense.

My lady's calling. She says she's hungry.

She's always hungry.

Day 795

There's an odor about my lady, like a dung heap on a hot day. If my script looks ill, it's because I closed my eyes as I wrote that. I shouldn't even think it. But she does—my lady does smell like hot dung.

Day 812

It's my honor to serve. It's my honor, I know it is, and yet . . . Ancestors, don't read this, but I begin to wonder, is it right? The lady is jailed for neglecting her duty, but I'm jailed for fulfilling mine.

I miss My Lord. The cat.

Day 834

Under, god of tricks, keeps thinking of new ways to bully us. I cooked our meal from a new sack of grain, one that was buried under crates and the rats hadn't yet touched. My stomach wasn't feeling round and open, so I only nibbled, but my lady ate any quantity of flat bread. She grumbles as she eats, like a beast feeding on short grass. Ancestors bless her.

After dinner, I noticed how colors seemed to wave around me, so intense I thought it was real. The bricks were orange and moved like fire, though there was no heat. Strangely, I didn't feel worried till my lady screamed and pointed up, where I only saw the wooden ceiling and darkness.

"It's coming down," she screamed. "It's falling in!"

"What is? What?"

Then she turned to the hole in the wall, screaming anew. "A wolf! A wolf eats through our wall!"

There was nothing there.

I held her and sang to her while she screamed and vomited. By the time my eyes no longer saw orange fire rippling over the bricks, my lady had collapsed into a soggy, though quiet, mess.

Bad grain. My mama warned me once that if eating stored grain makes you see things that aren't really there, then it's gone bad, touched by Under, god of tricks.

I suppose I should be grateful the bread didn't kill us, though it near killed me to have to dump the entire bag of grain out our hole.

Day 852

Sometimes I spend several hours by our hole calling to the guards. There's been no answer since the night the wolf howled. If Lord Khasar did kill them, why didn't my lady's father send others?

Day 912

I can hear the rats squeaking madly down there. When I'm half asleep, it sounds as though they're holding a party just to laugh at me. I can't sleep in the cellar again tonight. Though the smells from outside speak of spring, it still gets mighty cold, and my limbs are frozen by half, my jaw sore from chattering.

There are so many rats, I can't think what to do. I can't think much. I'm so cold from sleeping in the cellar, my head feels like ice, and I imagine that all the worry is cracking it. It's only been two years and a half. I call outside, shouting of how we've not much time and to send more food or please break us free. I have to think that no one's there. Maybe my lady's family doesn't care if we die, or even remember us at all.

Later

I've moved most of the remaining food up to our ground floor. It'll spoil faster out of the cold cellar, but at least the rats won't get it as easily. I've counted and measured, and we can't live four years on what the rats left behind. If I'm not too cold and tower-addled to do my figures, then we don't have enough to last a month.

I won't tell my lady. I don't think she'd understand. She barely speaks of late, barely notices me at all, even when I'm singing to her unknown ailment. Besides, I don't have the patience to hear her cry again.

Day 918

I've decided. We're going to live. It's such a relief! I begin to feel more my mucker self just to settle my mind on it. A mucker survives. No matter that we've not enough food. We'll find a way.

Day 920

Yesterday morning, I sat scraping at the mortar between two bricks. I didn't make breakfast. I didn't do the washing. I just scraped, scraped, scraped. I broke our kitchen knife. It never was a good knife, but now we've got none at all. Today I tried a wooden spoon and grated the handle down to its bowl. I'll keep trying everything till the wall breaks or my fingers do. So what if the guards are ordered to kill us on sight? They may not even be out there, and that death isn't as sure as the starving death awaiting us.

Just now, rat meat sounds as tasty as winter antelope.

Day 921

Rat meat is *not* tasty.

I managed to beat one senseless with my broom. I cut it up and served the stringy meat boiled. It's all right for a mucker to hunt rats when the yak stops giving milk enough for cheese, but no gentry should, Ancestors forgive me. The rat tasted dull and bitter, as if it had been eating mud, but my lady just chewed and chewed and swallowed. How could she not ask where the fresh meat came from? Sometimes I wonder if her brain was set upside down.

Day 925

Under, god of tricks, must love rats. They remember me and won't let my broom near. Over the past two days, I've hit myself more times than I've come close to a rat. I wish I had a bow and arrow to hunt with, but I left all those mucker tools behind.

You know something odd? Even though their appetites are killing us, I actually like those rats. It makes me smile to think of how brilliant they are at surviving. I think her khan would laugh with me about this.

Day 928

If my script wiggles, it's because my hand won't be steady. This is what I've been hearing, echoing into our tower through the broken hole.

"It was a lookout tower that doesn't look out anymore." A man's voice. "See here? Steps lead to nothing, and these bricks aren't as old as the rest. The door's been bricked up just like the windows."

"And who told you there's a lady inside?"

"Who didn't tell me? That's been the rumor for years."

Some laughter. "Then she's waiting for us, isn't she? Just ripe for the picking."

"I get first go."

A muffled thump.

"Don't use your shoulder, you yak head. That's solid bricking. Here, help me with that log. Mongke, Delger, come lend a hand!"

Later

It's been an hour I suppose, though it feels like days. The horrible knocking goes on, and I feel bruised just for hearing it. They move around the tower, testing the bricks, banging, trying to find a weak spot. Ancestors, after all my calling and praying, these are the men you send to break us out? Perhaps only Under heard me.

Forgive the wet marks here. I don't know if it comes from sweat or tears. My lady heard the banging and came to see what's happening. I didn't tell her what I heard the men say, but she guesses it's not her father come to beg pardon, guesses it's not her khan at rescue. I've set her in the cellar. She's a ball of trembling, the rats chittering around her. I told her to put her face in her knees when she cries so the men won't hear.

If they've come for a lady, they'll search the tower till she's found, I'd warrant. But maybe if they find me, they won't look too hard for another. Maybe they'll mistake me for the lady and leave when they're done. Carthen, goddess of strength, how I try to be brave! But I want to lock myself in the cellar, too. I want to run away. I don't want to see those men, I don't want what they'll do to me.

I make myself laugh, though silently, just thinking how I'll scratch them first. How I'll bite and tear at their eyes. I'll be more dangerous than a mad rat, and I'll fight just as hard to survive. I'm holding the shard of the kitchen knife in my left hand, a rag wrapped around one end so I can grip it fast. I will find their pig parts and cut them out before they touch me!

It was silent for minutes while I sketched. Now the battering again. I'm having trouble holding the brush.

Day 929

The wall still holds. How odd it is that, just now, that's a blessing.

Silence slumped against our door after the cold told us it was sundown. We slept with no fire, my lady and I tight together on the same mattress, too scared to climb back into the cellar because the ladder squeaks. In the tar black dark she begged me for a fire, but if the men see smoke in the chimney they'll know we're here, they won't give up then. I know why she begged, though it might've meant death. Even though we've spent three years in near dark, the total black scared me more than the thought of mud fever or even Lord Khasar. The total black filled my eyes and nostrils and throat and felt like forever.

Now, daylight noses through the broken hole, around the last bag of dried peas I jammed in front of it. I warmed ink and water in my hands enough to write. I have naught to say. I'm just looking for comfort in words.

I wish I had a cat curled up in my lap, his sleep purr singing that everything is all right.

Another thought spins and spins in my head. If those men couldn't break our wall, what chance have we?

Day 930

A silent day. No fire. We chewed dried peas and drank water. Every moment I expect to hear another knock. I wonder if those men are crouching nearby, waiting to pounce at our first sound.

Day 931

The men haven't returned, or else they're removed from our tower, waiting for us to appear. It doesn't matter. We have to get out.

I spent the day chipping at the mortar around the dump hole, hoping that area was weaker than others. I used our pot lid, as the knife is now use-less. No more voices, except the squeak of rats and my own scrape, scrape, scrape. The barrels are nearly empty, the last of the salted meat is reeking with rot. Even without rats and my lady's appetite, we wouldn't have lasted seven years unless her honored father had brought us fresh food. Now, we have just days left.

I pray to Evela, goddess of sunshine, bring us into your light again. Ris, god of roads and towns, let us find home. Vera, goddess of food, give us enough to eat. Goda, goddess of sleep, use your skill on Under so his tricks won't touch us. And Carthen, goddess of strength, make me strong enough to break down the walls.

We're not going to die. I already decided.

Day 932

Just hours ago a wonder occurred.

I was lying on my straw mattress. I was asleep, mostly, though I was still aware of my lady snoring. Forgive me, Ancestors, but it's the truth — my lady snores like a ram with a cold. And that wasn't the wonder.

I was dreaming of the rats. These past months, I dream asleep and I dream awake. Often I'm not sure which is sleep and which is madness, just as I'm never certain when it's noonday or deep night.

In the dream, I could see through the floor into the cellar, down to the ragged, silvery shapes of the rats scurrying. I saw them nosing along the cellar floor, finding a fallen grain here, a bit of wax from a cheese wheel there. Then I saw them climb some empty crates and leave the tower.

The dream shocked me awake, and I sat up.

"The rats got into the tower," I said, right to the darkness. "That means the rats can get out."

I lit a candle in the fire and crept down the cellar ladder. Little eyes looked back at me in the dark. One scuttled away, and I followed. It disappeared behind some crates, but I heard the sound of its claws as it climbed. I stepped onto an empty barrel and held my candle up close to the place where the wall and ceiling meet. This is what I saw.

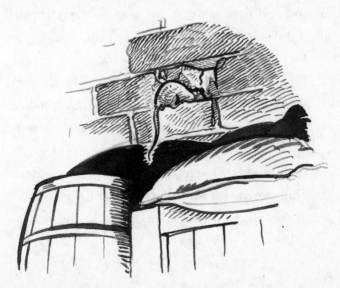

I gave the area a hearty shove. The wall moaned. I hit it again. I tore a slat of wood from a barrel and wedged out a brick, then attacked it with my fists. I started to feel good striking the wall, and I got a little angry, too. The anger felt like a stinging breath of late autumn air after sitting by a hot fire.

I don't know how long I fought with the bricks, but my hands were bruised and my shoulders ached something powerful. The rats got out of my way. I guess they knew I wasn't fooling around.

Now there was a hole big enough for a girl. For me. Night air whooshed down into the cellar and tasted like grass. I stood there and just breathed. I guess I should admit, I was a little scared to leave.

But eventually I did put my hands through the hole and feel level earth, I did crawl up onto hard ground and fight my way out of some nasty shrubs, and I did stand on real dirt and look up.

I was outside. I was under the stars.

I breathed in as if it were the first time I'd breathed in years. My body felt stripped naked, washed hard in cold water, dried, and dressed again.

I was under the stars, like a fish is under water.

Tomorrow we'll leave the tower. If the guards are out there, ready to shoot an arrow at the mucker maid escaping, or the knocking men wait to do terrible things, then know, Ancestors, that I did my best. I tried to do my duty.

And save my lady, who once said that her mucker maid was her best friend.

PART 2

The Adventure Thereafter

Day 1

I decided to start numbering the days at one again to mark the time when we began anew.

I was up all last night. Who can sleep when there's real air to breathe? Who can sleep when there's a sky? Still, I thought it wise to let my lady rest as long as she could, so for hours I kept company with the stars. When I couldn't stand to wait another moment, I clambered back inside, wrote in this book, and then woke her with the news.

She seemed happy. She seemed relieved. But at the hole in the cellar, she waffled. She said she couldn't climb up it, she said her ankle hurt, she said the hole was too small, she said anything to stay inside. After some time of this, I guess I got a bit tetchy and, Ancestors forgive me, I ordered her like I would a sulky sheep, pushing her from behind. I thought all she needed was to feel that glorious night air, but when I scrambled out behind her, I found her clinging to the side of the tower and shaking like a cornered rabbit.

I put my arms around her to make her feel tight and safe. I said, "Breathe the air, my lady! Look at the stars!" But she just shook.

Thinking it was the darkness of night that haunted her, I waited for the sun to come up. It was nearly dawn. The sky brightened in the east, turning white, yellow, then blue. It was perfect. I hadn't realized that by firelight, nothing in the tower had shown true colors. All we saw for years was black, gray, and orange.

My lady kept her eyes squeezed shut.

"Look, my lady. Open your eyes and see the colors."

It was the wrong moment, for just as she peeked, the first edge of sun rose over the horizon to peek back at her.

My lady screamed and fell to the earth. "The sun burst! We're going to burn up!"

"It's just so bright, I think, because we're used to darkness. We'll grow accustomed to it in time."

But she insisted that she was burning and rolled around, screaming and thrashing at nothing.

I dragged her inside.

We'll try again tomorrow.

Day 3

We've spent the past two days taking little steps out of the tower, shielding our eyes and looking around, then crawling back in. My lady tries to be brave, and she bites her lip and cries silently, sure she's on fire, but I tell her it's just the normal sun, that Evela, goddess of sunlight, will protect us. I've sung the song for good courage and the song for clear thought so many times, I feel hoarse and drained, as though the words plucked out my own courage and thoughts and tossed the rest of me aside like grain husks.

There are no guards with strung bows aimed at the escaping maid—at least I think there aren't since I'm still alive, but I can't yet see past my outstretched hand, not with the sun shooting bright arrows into my eyes.

Last night we sat under the moon for a long while, and my lady finally breathed in and sighed and seemed happy to be in the air again. She never once let go of my arm.

I spent this afternoon in the tower washing, making bundles of our blankets to carry spare clothing, and baking barley bread stuck with peas from the barrel scrapings. We'll leave tomorrow. I've packed brushes and ink enough, so I can keep writing of how we fare. I hope there will be much to tell.

Day 5

Oh, I feel so low, I want to curl up in the dirt and just moan, moan, moan. Everyone's gone. Everything's burned.

We knew from afar that something wasn't right. There should've been people passing us on the road to her father's city. The sun was so piercing I couldn't see much, but all the world felt wrong, as if the road appeared flat but was actually as steep as a mountain, as if we'd died in the tower and were just ghosts wandering a shadow world.

My lady wouldn't look up. I draped a blanket over her head and she stumbled along, her eyes on her feet.

"Would you like to go back to your father?" I asked.

"He won't have me. And even if he would, I won't have him." She gripped my arm as if without me she'd drown dead in the sunlight.

"We can't live out in the open like this," I said, "not for long, not without a gher. We need to—"

"It doesn't matter where we go. Lord Khasar will find me and wed me and then kill me."

"It won't come to that, my lady. If you won't go home, I'll take you to Song for Evela and reunite you with your khan."

"No! I won't see him."

"But he's your love," I said. "He'll take right care of you."

My lady had stopped walking and stood in the center of the road, hunched and shivering.

"He won't." Her voice went raspy soft and strange as she said, "He wants to kill me with arrows and knives."

Well, those words nearly knocked my feet out from under me. "Khan Tegus wants to kill you? Why would you think that?"

"I heard the whispers."

I nearly laughed as I asked, "Voices whispered to you that Khan Tegus wants to murder you with arrows and knives?"

She looked at me then, her eyes clearing a bit, and said, "No, I didn't hear anything. I just don't want to see Khan Tegus anymore. That's all."

My guess is that she's tower-addled something fierce, her brain awry in her head and her understanding tilted steep. But it's not proper for me to make decisions for her. So what's a mucker maid to do?

We slept the night under a tree, my lady's back

pressed to the trunk. I lay awake for hours, playing a game, trying to keep my gaze on the black parts of the sky, but my focus couldn't help but slide back to those bright stars. My eyes wanted the light. I breathed in as though I'd drink the sky cold. It was a good night.

Then this morning we approached her honored father's city. I saw a gray smudge that must've been the wall, but there was a dark spot that didn't seem right. As soon as we were close enough to make out details, I gasped right out loud. My lady looked up then and saw it, too.

"There's a hole in the wall," she said. "Someone broke the wall."

We kept approaching but stayed in the shadows of the trees that line the road, though they didn't feel any safer. The city gate was gone. Torn out? Burned?

"I don't understand," she said in her little-girl tone. "If something happened to the gate, shouldn't there be workers to fix it? And there used to be gate guards. Didn't there?"

She started to cry, and we had to stop. I held her head to my shoulder, rocking her, rubbing her back. Poor thing, I don't think she knows where to put the whole world.

We lay down under a tree and I sang a soothing song, one for deep sleep that goes, "Trout in the water, deep underwater, swimming so silver." She succumbed to sleep, and I left her in the shade and crept toward the city. Not only was there a hole in the wall, but the entire length was marred with black marks. Arrow shafts stuck between stones.

As I climbed atop the heaping rubble, a striped snake startled beneath my foot. It didn't attack, just swam deeper into the stones. The snake was surely a sign of something, though I'm not sure what. All creatures belong to Titor, god of animals, but the snake is the favorite beast of Under, god of tricks.

When I'd climbed high enough on the wall, I finally witnessed the whole truth of it. Her honored father's city is no more. It's razed, gutted, gone. No sounds. Even the smoke from the burning has blown away. I could see heaps of stone, charred wood, broken wagons. No people.

Qadan and Mistress. All the folk in my lady's house, her father, sister, brother. That city that teemed with people, all gone. All dead?

A cat passed me and meowed as though nothing were wrong in the world. My heart tipped up in hope that it was My Lord, but this cat's fur was brown and white. She didn't come when I sang. I guess she'd been a wild cat for too long and no longer craved the company of people.

I've had time to write, as my lady has slept all of the night and most of the day. We have just a day's worth of the flat bread left, so I need to scavenge more food, but if I'm not by my lady's side when she wakes, she screams. I braid her hair as tightly as I can without pulling loose her scalp, making sure every hair crisscrosses another. I sing, sing, sing every song I know and I even make up a few. But my lady's not well. She is not well.

Day 6

Is her khan's land burned down as well? Is everyone gone? Maybe we're the last living souls in the world and we'll drift from tree shade to tree shade, eating grass and speaking with snakes and cats until we're stooped from age and crumble into the dust. Today I keep thinking of all the people who have left and never returned—my brothers, Khan Tegus, our guards, this entire city. What a strange, dark world that swallows people whole.

I need to know if anyone still lives. The not knowing makes me queasy. My lady said she won't go to Song for Evela, but Ancestors forgive me, I'm going to take her anyway. She won't ask where we're going, and once she arrives and sees her khan, she'll heal and forget the whispers.

Before we journey, I should go into the city. We need food, and we need vessels to carry water in case we can't follow a stream. My lady fares a bit better today after many songs of healing. If I can coax her, she'll come with me. She knows her home and may find stashes of food that pillagers would leave behind. I'll admit, I'm afraid to go in to the city. If an army did this, then warriors may still lurk there.

And if the Ancestors did this, if in anger they wiped the land clean, then why did they let my lady and me live? Did they forget about us, locked away, hidden from the gaze of the Eternal Blue Sky?

I just looked back at the beginning of my writings and the title I gave this book of thoughts. It's all wrong now. I named it so, thinking that we would be seven years in the tower, and the idea of having an adventure thereafter gave me hope. I'm a stubborn mare sometimes and must dangle my own carrot. Here we are two and a half years later, saved from one coffin only to find my lady's city is but a second. My title is no longer correct. Two and a half years is not seven, but I'll leave it. I don't like the look of scratched-out letters.

Day 7

My lady came with me into the city, Ancestors bless her. She shook like a thin tree caught in a wind, but she came.

I don't fault her—there was much to shake at. Not a roof left intact, not a soul alive. And many a body, burned bones, some still stuck with arrows, some missing skulls. I won't describe any more because, truth be told, I don't want to frighten my own self.

The whole place was so still, I longed to find living people. But at the same time, every moment I feared running into another soul. There could be warriors or the knocking men, and I have nothing to defend us with but my own fingernails. Every shadow, every corner seemed dangerous. The dread was so powerful, I felt like I was walking on my own studded rat traps. Even the breeze hurt against my skin.

I can't say which is more terrible, to be locked

away from everyone or to be free in a world where all are dead. Both are different shades of darkness.

When we came at last to my lady's house, we stood and just stared. How grand it had been! So lovely and large my mama wouldn't have believed the tale. Now it was a heap of stones, green roof tiles, and cinder. My lady didn't cry. She didn't even shake. I think she hadn't had much happiness in that house.

My lady was able to point me to the spots where the kitchen had stood and the likely location of the food cellars. While I sorted through the rubble, she stared.

"Maybe it never really existed. Maybe this is all it ever was."

"No, my lady. It was real."

"I can't remember. . . ." Her gaze didn't stray from the heap of rubble. "I can't remember, Dashti. Are you sure?"

Sometimes my lady asks me questions that I can't answer with any degree of patience.

From under the lighter rubble, I pulled out a sack half full of barley meal, some rope, a large ceramic pot with just the spout broken, a wheel of cheese still covered in wax, a jar of oil with its cork intact, and three boots. By then my arms were too tired to lift a pebble, so I wandered around the ruins, scanning for a gleam of anything useful. By the Ancestors' luck, eventually I did find a knife. With that tool I can sharpen sticks to dig roots, spear fish and rodents, and gut them for the eating. It gave me a bit of hope.

I hadn't realized how silent all the world was until I heard a cry that made my stomach jump up into my throat. I thought warriors had found us, that we were dog's meat for sure. But then I saw.

Titor, god of animals, must've taken pity on us and sent a gift for the last lady of Titor's Garden.

At first the animal looked ready to bolt, but I sang the yak song, the one that bubbles up your chest and says, "He laughs, he laughs, he moans and laughs." I've never seen any creature respond so quickly to an animal song. He came to me at a near trot and stuck his muzzle right in my palm. This one's made of the friendly stuff.

I named him Mucker, and he's the handsomest yak I ever saw, with his coat a glossy brownish black, horns so long and proud as to make any she-yak blush, and grand teeth all still intact. He's so strong, carrying our few possessions must feel like a fly landed on his back. Yaks are the best animals for travel and will eat whatever stubby greens the road will produce. Give me one good yak over a herd of horses any day.

And what fine company he is! He nuzzles my hands and lips my ears, he stands close to me as we walk, sometimes pressing his broad head against my side, his horn wrapped around my back like an arm. I think he has a wonderful sense of humor, too. I told him a few stories and he turned his ears, listening heartily. Just writing about him lifts my mouth into a smile. Mucker and I will get along fine.

Day 8

This landscape is as familiar to me as the inside of my eyelids. West of the city, the terrain eases back into the steppes—stretches of grass growing as tall as my knees, low, rounded hills, stripes of streams carrying away the mountains' snow, and the occasional knotty tree, wind-whipped and bending.

I'd forgotten how the wind never sleeps out here. The clean air moving against my skin was more delicious than spiced food—at first. But when we stopped for the night, I couldn't fall asleep for all the memories of mucker life the smell of the wind thrust into my mind.

When I did finally sleep, I dreamed I'd been running through the ruined city, trying to find a way out. When I went into a house, I found it full of bodies, and before I could turn away, the walls sealed up around me. Goda, goddess of sleep, save me from such visions. Even after I woke, the dream still felt sticky, clinging to me as if I'd walked through a spider's web. I'm lying against Mucker now and feeling a bit easier for his warmth and sleepy grunts.

Stars light my page. We'll be starting our journey in earnest come dawn and I suppose I won't have a chance to write again for some time. Song for Evela is west of Titor's Garden, so we'll follow the road that stretches toward the setting sun. If it would take two weeks for the khan's party with their horses and decent supplies, for us, I guess it'll be more than twice that. We don't have food enough, but it's spring and there are trout in the stream. If there's something a mucker knows, it's how to eat from nothing. No walls trap us now!

The smell of grass and yak is making me drunk with wishes that I'd never left the steppes—but after Mama died, I didn't know how to survive alone. Did I give up everything to learn to make letters and words on paper?

No. I'm a lady's maid. She would've died in that tower without me, I know that. My worth lies in keeping my lady alive for her khan. The Ancestors will honor such a life as mine. I hope.

Day 33

Three weeks we've been walking and still not another soul. We spotted the remains of some villages, but whether the folk there fled when the city was destroyed or whether they were all killed, too, I don't know.

A few days ago we forded a wide river, and I believe it must be the one that marks the border of Titor's Garden and Song for Evela. If so, then we've crossed into her khan's realm. Will we find the city gutted and full of the dead unburied? Never mind, I'd rather not think on that question.

My lady's clothes begin to hang on her again. I get her off Mucker's back and walking as often as she'll allow, so her blood is moving and her breath is exhaling the tower poison from her body. But oft times she must ride, for she's so beset by darkness as to not see the road.

This morning she began to scream, "I'm drowning, I can't breathe. The air's not right, I can't breathe." She clawed at the air and grabbed her throat, and

125

when my songs of healing did her little good, I found a hollowed overhang by the stream and stuck her inside. She calmed at once.

I'm sitting outside the little cave, where I can still see the sky, where the sunlight moves on my arms. Being inside that tiny space, even for a moment, that's what made me want to scream.

While she's been napping, I've combed Mucker's shedding hair with my fingers, sharpened a new stick, boiled the sting out of some nettle leaves, then speared a fish in the stream, wrapped it in leaves, stuffed it with nettles, and cooked it in coals. The smell of fish cooking is rich enough to wake up the trees, but still my lady sleeps.

So I ate my portion and then lay on my back, watching the clouds. Seven years of food isn't worth trading for the sky.

Day 41

Others live!

Since fording the river, the steppes have faded away, trees and then great woods taking over. Today we reached a crossroads and saw a group of traders traveling the north-south road. They were whole and living and speaking—real people, not ghosts. What a heavenly sight.

"How far is the city?" I asked when we were upon them. I didn't say Song for Evela, for my lady still doesn't know where we're going.

"Four days, if you walk straight. You weren't coming from the east just now, were you?"

"Sure enough, they're coming in from Titor's Garden," said another trader, then he leaned over and laughed hard.

The first rolled his eyes. "Hmph, very funny. As though anything comes from Titor's Garden."

"What happened there?" I asked.

"Lord Khasar happened. Wiped it out entirely almost a year ago. Now he's off making war with Goda's Second Gift. We're hoping he burns them down, too."

"Hoping?"

"As should you. If he just conquers, if he adds their armies to his, all the warriors of our realm will have little chance against him. He's bound to come our way next. Tales be true, there's nowhere in all the Eight Realms where Lord Khasar's shadow won't cross."

My lady's hands covered her face, her shoulders trembling.

Day 44

Our grain meal is long gone, as is the cheese and oil, and after days on nothing but nettles, I think we were both feeling twig-thin and cranky. This morning I killed a marmot with my stick. I stuffed its belly full of hot coals and let it cook from the inside out. We had no salt or spice, and the meat was so tough it took fifty chews each bite, but even so I guess I never ate a meal so delicious. Even my lady didn't complain.

Very soon, I'll reunite her with her khan. And then? If she wishes, I'll stay with her and be nurse-maid to her babies. If not, I'll find work in the city, or perhaps I will return to the steppes and find a mucker clan, take a seven-year oath, and work in their herds in exchange for eating their meals and sleeping on the floors of their ghers. But I'd be twenty-five by the time I was eligible to marry, and that's old for a mucker bride, even if anyone would take me without a dowry.

I'll worry about it after I see my lady settled in her happiness.

The sky no longer seems breathlessly huge, but feels to press down on me. Perhaps I'm just afraid of the uncertainty to come. When I'm moving on a journey, the ending is still unknown and possibly wonderful. But once I arrive, it's hard to keep imagining.

Day 46

Ris, god of roads and towns, has guided our feet, for we are here at last! The city of Song for Evela is greater than Titor's Garden, with a wall three-men high and a small army on horseback beside each gate. They fear Lord Khasar, I think.

A caravan from the south entered the gate ahead of us. I'd seen caravans arrive in Titor's Garden when I ran errands for Qadan, and I knew that they offer their goods to the lord or lady of the city before setting up in the market. Following behind seemed the fastest path to finding the house of my lady's khan.

It was a bold sight, camels and wagons and dozens of traders swathed in the brilliant white cloth of the desert lands. They uncovered their cargo to excite interest in buyers, and I caught glimpses of dye pots, porcelain bowls, bolts of silk, casks of honey, bags of sugar, skins of wine, and bricks of incense. The incense and the scented woods wafted a heavenly scent over us, and I walked as though in a dream. Performers rode atop the cargo, their heads bare and painted faces smiling. Later they'll show off their talents in the market to attract buyers to the goods. Acrobats, contortionists, storytellers with wild, strange accents—I wish I could see them perform.

We followed the caravan up the streets, past the wooden houses, merchant stalls, and animal pens, toward the city center where the buildings are made of stone. It wasn't long before my heart was going as fast as a rabbit's stomp. I was wondering if her khan would be in his house, if we'd see him that very hour. If he'd welcome her back, if he'd take her in and marry her at once. And what would happen to me then?

The streets were clean and straight, as different from the crooked, narrow lanes of Titor's Garden as my lady's face is from my own. And as I ached for a way to tell her where we really were, she said, "This is Song for Evela, isn't it?"

"Yes, my lady."

Her face wrinkled as though she were pained.

"Khan Tegus isn't plotting to kill you," I said. "I spoke with him in the tower, remember? He is goodness from boots to eyebrows, my lady, I could tell that, plain as plain. The tower sits heavily on you still, that's all. And the whispers—"

"I don't hear any whispers," she snapped. "I'm fine. I'm not afraid."

She walked tall, her hand on Mucker's back, her other arm in mine. She was trying to be brave, I could see. And it twisted my heart.

She didn't say another word for all those long, straight streets. Perhaps she felt buried in all that life. I certainly did. There were people everywhere—cooking in the street, shouting and chasing, throwing wash water out the window, fighting and kissing and eating and just talk, talk, talking. The smells! And the noise, like having your head stuck inside a wasp's nest. I'd forgotten that people were so loud, that they move around so much. They were beautiful, their eyes, their hands, their voices and laughs. It was many blocks through the city before I realized I'd been crying and I didn't even know why. Is that strange? I think Mama would understand. And maybe Khan Tegus.

Her khan's house was fat and square, with a roof five tiers high made of yellow and blue enamel tiles, grander even than my lady's house had been. How can anyone believe such a claim? And yet it's true. A throng of guards stood at posts all around, and more clustered about the gate. We tried to enter, but they stopped us and a little man in a deel too long for his feet asked us our business.

"Tell them who you are," I said.

"No," said my lady.

I spoke in her ear so the little man wouldn't over-hear.

"Please, my lady. Tell them you are Lady Saren of Titor's Garden, betrothed of Khan Tegus. Tell them so you can be fit up like gentry and live as you should."

"No. And I forbid you to tell anyone who I am." She was looking around now like a hunted thing. "Lord Khasar would find me, or Khan Tegus would—"

"He won't hurt you, my lady! He'll protect you."

Her eyes were wet, her chin quivered. "What if he's not safe, as I once thought? No one is, but you." She gripped both my arms with her hands, like a bird clutches a branch.

"I can't look after you forever," I whispered. "I don't have money or work, and I don't have status or clan. We're barely surviving, my lady. And come winter, we'll freeze and die without a gher. You're an honored lady. You need more than a mucker maid can give you. Please, tell them who you are."

My lady took a breath, turned to the little man, and said, "I'm a mucker."

Ancestors forgive me, but I think I cracked in half then. I turned my face into Mucker's neck and I cried and cried like a roof in the rain. I was so tired. Not just of walking or feeling hungry, or washing and keeping my lady. I was just tired of being Dashti, of breathing, of being alive. *Forgive me, Mama.*

"What's going on here?" A white-haired woman approached the little man. I found out later that her name is Shria. "Who are these girls blocking the way?"

The little man cleared his throat as if to signal us to leave. I took a deep breath and felt my heart stutter and my sobbing dry up, and I knew I couldn't be broken any more than I was. There's some comfort in that. Mucker was lipping the laces on my boot, and I thought, I can get by, and I can find a way to keep my lady alive, but I promised poor Mucker he'd have a stable and a brush down at the end of our journey.

So I wiped my cheeks and told Shria, "I bring a

gift for Khan Tegus. This is the best yak I've ever known. His name's Mucker."

The little man started to protest. "We don't buy animals from—"

"No, not buy. I want the khan to have him. It's an honest gift from a mucker girl."

It was a right stupid thing to do, I know, and as I sit here writing, I can't believe I was so thick-skulled as to give away our only possession. With no animal or tent, in a few months' time winter would whack us dead like a yak's tail slaps a fly. I might've traded him for employment at the least. But in that moment I only thought how much I loved that yak, what warm and happy company he had been for me when I thought all the world was dead, and how he deserved a stall like the kind her khan's house was sure to have. And a little I thought of her khan. He gave us My Lord the cat, who was the best cat who ever breathed. And though Khan Tegus never came back for us, I'd heard the sound of his soul through his voice, and I believe he's the kind of person who deserves the best yak in all the realms.

I kissed Mucker's nose and sang into his huge ear the song to ease parting, the one that goes, "Roads go straight and roads go on, my heart moves like the sun." A boy came to lead him away to promises of

oats and that quickly Mucker was gone. I hadn't realized it would hurt to lose that yak, but I nearly gasped
at the pain in my heart. Thank the Ancestors, Shria
didn't give me the chance to think and mourn because
she asked right quick, "Do you girls know kitchen
work?"

I showed her my hands. She turned them over,
felt for calluses.

"She's a good girl," she said to the little man.
"Her face has the mark of bad luck, doesn't it? Even
so, I'd bet my shoes she's a good girl."

"What about the other one?" The little man
squinted at my lady.

I smelled hope in the air, and I snatched at it.
"She's my clan sister, and we've survived in harsher
living than most girls could imagine. Why, she's worth
two of any city girl you can find."

I guess they believed me because here we are in
her khan's house. Instead of placing my lady in a
chamber of silk and pillows, as I'd hoped to do, she's
sharing my blanket on the kitchen floor by the washing hearth.

Ancestors but I'm tired and kitchen work starts
at dawn. I'll pay for this writing time tomorrow.

Day 54

Though it's middle night, I'll write now because I never have other time. I'm used to recording my thoughts by the ghost light of fire, anyhow.

This kitchen is like a herd of wild horses for how it runs and runs and never stops but to sleep. My lady and I tend the wash fire, boil water, scrub pots, and wash aprons and rags. There are two other scrubber girls that share our fire, and we all sleep together before it, using the dirty rags for pillows, or one another's legs and bellies. I'll tell you somewhat of the other girls.

Gal is thirteen and our youngest. Her eyes are pale brown and so sad. She's from Goda's Second

Gift, and her mother made her flee before Lord Khasar's armies arrived. Because of the mountain range to the west, she had to sneak southeast through Thoughts of Under and the ruins of Titor's Garden before finding safety here. She doesn't know where her family is or if they still live. At night, I hear her cry, but she's camel stubborn and won't let us comfort her. When she doesn't suspect what I'm about, I work close to her and sing the song for heartache. She's got a wicked tongue and quick temper and saves it all for my lady, who is a slow worker.

Qacha is eighteen like me, and what's more, she's a mucker! Her mama was in the city of Titor's Garden when Khasar attacked, but her papa survived, and he works in the stables. They have the same half day free each week and spend it outside the city walls, talking and hunting for roots and berries. We teach each other new songs and talk about the steppes. How she laughs! She laughs when she wakes, and laughs when they dump another load of washing before us, and laughs when Cook knocks her head with a spoon for spilling water.

I love Qacha like I love sunshine, but I don't seek her company more often than I must. When we laugh together, I see how my lady looks, her eyes cast down, as though she wishes she could curl up and cry.

I don't call her my lady in front of others, of course. Her name here is Sar, and she wears her braid down like all the scrubber girls. We say that she's my clan sister, since we don't look enough alike to claim the same mother. Clan sisters. Ancestors forgive me.

Day 60

This lie is making me feel heavy, as though all the world is under water and I can't run for its weight. I can't be a good scrubber because I'm looking after my lady. I can't be a good lady's maid because I'm scrubbing pots and rags. I'm failing at both and I hate it like I've never hated a thing in my life.

And my lady isn't well. She doesn't cry so often as

she did on our journey, but she still hangs like a willow in leaf. Always she stays near me, seizing my arm or standing so close our sides touch. She looks about as if everything in the world had teeth and was planning to bite her. She weeps at night more than Gal.

"Is it the work, my lady?" I asked her tonight, when we were cracking soap from the block in the cellar.

"I'm tired," she said. "I don't like Cook. I want to go to sleep."

"You don't have to be a scrubber anymore, my lady. Your khan is the master here. Go to him and remind him of your powerful love."

She turned white and shook like a hare facing a hunter. I patted her face and shook her and prodded her with my toes, but she wouldn't agree, she just stood there, dumb and shaking. Ancestors pardon me, but I dumped wash water over her head.

My lady was angry. "Why did you do that?"

"To wake you up! To make you make sense. Tell me, my lady. Why won't you go to him? Why?"

"I don't want to say. You won't believe me. But I know it, I know they all want me dead. And if one doesn't kill me, the other will. Lord Khasar will come after me. He's a beast and he tears out the throats of goats with his teeth. I saw him."

"Oh, my lady," I said, and turned my back so she couldn't see my expression. First she claimed Khan Tegus is plotting to kill her with arrows and knives and now Lord Khasar bites goats. In her mind, I don't think she's ever left the tower. She's still seeing things that aren't there.

Day 62

The girls at the next fire wash plates and platters and occasionally help Cook with the stirring. Sometimes they say things about us pot scrubbers, or about my mottled face and my lady's slowness. It makes Gal glare and Qacha hold her laughter. Maybe before the tower, such talk would have made me feel low, but I have no patience for it now. The world is far too beautiful to waste a moment on such nonsense. Even so, we four scrubber girls keep to ourselves.

Except there is one boy who's a cutter—that is, he cuts up vegetables, prepares meat, that sort of kitchen work. Well, he had some free time and he came and helped me scrub pots. *In his free time*. Then today we caught eyes as we worked and he winked. I giggled about it with Qacha, but I don't know what to think. His name's Osol and he has loads of hair and a fine jaw. Maybe he hasn't noticed my skin splotches? How could he not notice? All the same, I keep the left side of my face turned away from him whenever I can.

I haven't heard any gossip about Khan Tegus. Or Lord Khasar.

Day 64

Today was my free half day, but Saren had to work. I wasn't going to leave her, she's likely to fall apart without me nearby, but the girls insisted.

"Go have some freedom," said Qacha, walking me to the door. "You haven't taken a half day since you arrived."

"But Sar—"

Gal grumbled. "That girl works slower than a snail makes a trail. Let her get kicked out of the kitchens already."

"Never mind," said Qacha. "She'll be fine. I'll watch Sar. Go on!"

It felt so nice to have someone looking after me a bit, and I believed Saren would be just fine with a solid mucker girl like Qacha watching out for her. So I left.

It was strange walking about without my lady

hanging on my side. Ancestors forgive me, but I felt as though someone cut me loose from heavy chains. First I went to the market. A caravan visited the khan's house two days ago, and I hoped to view some splendid performers.

Sadly, this caravan had only one contortionist and all he did was stand on his head and occasionally wiggle his legs, so I moved on, gliding my hand over the finery for sale — bundles of cinnabar, camphor, and sandalwood, bags of brown and white sugar, pearls and purple gems safe under glass, fragrant waxes in square bundles, turquoise, pink coral, and my favorite — blue nuggets of lapis lazuli.

I was gazing at the blue stones when I heard the caravan storyteller's magnificent voice. She boomed during the dramatic bits and then went low and eerie to make your hairs rise. The desert folk don't know the Ancestors and their tales, so the stories she told were foreign to me. Stories of night and fear, some so strange they left me feeling shrouded in ghosts.

One was like the story of the skinwalkers that I'd heard before — people who deal with the desert shamans to gain animal powers, but the storyteller added more details than I'd ever heard. First, a skinwalker offers his spirit as barter to a desert shaman, then he must kill a close relative — the more he loves the person he kills, the greater his power will be. Imagine such a thing! After that sacrifice, the desert shaman summons a predator spirit into the person, who then gains the added strength and cunning of that beast as well as the ability change into its shape. The storyteller told of man-leopards that prowl the desert night and with one bite turn a living person into a corpse.

My mouth went dry and I wanted to cover my ears, but I sat and listened anyway. Could it be true? Only the shamans should have power to change into animals, as foxes in service of the Ancestors. Shouldn't they?

It was a dark story and I needed lightening, so I headed back to the khan's house and visited Mucker in the stables. That magnificent yak grunted happily and snorted over my hands, leaving them warm and somewhat sticky. I sang to him and brushed him, and he looked shiny as polished wood when I left.

Here I am out in the sunshine, a full hour left for me to just sit and smile. Osol passed by, making a run to the dairy, and he dropped a wildflower on my book. I called out a greeting as he scurried away, and he looked back at me and winked. And smiled. He has a smile to be proud of.

The sky is a yawning blue, big and delicious, as though it wants me to be happy.

Later

Saren didn't do quite as well as I'd hoped. She panicked, there was some screaming, and they had to stuff her in a closet before Cook heard.

"She threw a tantrum like a waddling child," was how Qacha explained it. "I don't know how you put up with her."

"She's had a time of it," I said. "She lost her family."

"Who hasn't?"

I couldn't explain about the tower, and about Saren being gentry and made of softer stuff than muckers. But are they? I mean, her khan is gentry and it makes me smile to imagine him throwing a tantrum. Would Saren be like Tegus if I could heal whatever ails her? Then again, didn't the Ancestors make gentry perfect? And if they did, what about Lord Khasar?

I'm not sure about any of it anymore, and that's the truth.

Day 67

Today Qacha, Saren, and I were sitting on the floor scrubbing pots, and we mucker girls got to reminiscing about the steppes. Living every day under the Eternal Blue Sky, surrounded by animals, milking in the mornings, making cheese and yogurt, washing and cooking and cleaning, and then running free through the grass like antelope. I can still imagine myself in that life, as clearly as if I'm eight and in two braids, drinking milk fresh from the mare and twisting dry grass into play dolls.

"I never, ever imagined, not for a moment, that I wouldn't stay there forever," I said.

Qacha nodded. "We had a nice herd of sheep and my father would tell me, 'You see that lamb there? That one will be part of your dowry. And that one, too.' But then Khasar attacked, and we were camped too near the city, and his men stole animals and scattered the rest and killed . . . well, never mind. But before the attack, I thought I'd marry some mucker boy within the year." She laughed at that, all pleasantness again.

"And now here we are," I said, scraping some slop out of the pot and flinging it into the fire.

For a time we scrubbed in silence, then Qacha asked, "Would you go back right now if you could?"

I tried to see my lady without looking at her. She was elbow deep in her pot, but her face was earnest, as if she might be listening. I wished I could tell Qacha, *I'm trapped. I've taken an oath. Sar is actually an honored lady, the Ancestors made me from mud to serve her. I can't leave her. She's a bird with a broken wing. She needs me.*

But I said, "It's an odd thing to live all your life in one place and then lose it forever. It's a strange thing not to know if I'll ever be a mama like my own."

Qacha just nodded. She's a good one, that Qacha. She seems to sense when to keep talking and when to let the words drizzle into silence.

Day 69

I'm in the root cellar with a candle, and Cook doesn't know. I should be scrubbing, but I have to write now so I can stop shaking.

146

Earlier when we'd worked through all the dirty pots, Cook had us wash some deels for the serving girls. When the clothing was dried and folded, she sent me and Gal to deliver them to the other side of the house. We walked down those long corridors, all fit tight with stone floors, the walls snug with tapestries over carved wood, windows set with glass, porcelain bowls resting on lacquered tables, the most beautiful place I'd ever been. We hooked arms as we went, both afraid and elated to be walking freely through such grandeur. She can be a nice girl sometimes, that Gal, she's just sadder than the last lamb.

We passed by the doorway to the feast hall, and what a sight! Glass windows in all colors, a ceiling so high someone on horseback couldn't reach it when stretching.

Then up ahead three men were walking. Toward us. One was younger than the rest.

"I saw him my first day here," whispered Gal. "That's Khan Tegus."

Khan Tegus. That was his face! Those were the shoulders, the arms, the chest, the whole being of the man who once was no more than a boot, hands, and a voice. Thinking of our talks, of the laughing parts, of My Lord the cat and the pine bough, it was hard not to shout hello. I nearly rushed forward to greet him as family does, gripping forearms, touching cheeks, smelling his neck to invite in the breath of his soul.

And then I remembered how I gave him my own shirt. If he knew what I'd done, how I pretended to be my lady, he could hang me on the south wall.

His face seemed a kettle of worry, those men talking at him as they walked, and I wished I could hold his hand and sing him some ease. As he passed us, the corridor didn't feel so wide anymore. His sleeve brushed mine.

He looked at me, for barely a moment.

Only just now did I realize what I should've done—tell him at once that Lady Saren is here. Or *is* that what I should've done? Is it my duty to obey my lady or to do what's best for her? Nibus, god of order, direct my thoughts.

Day 70

Why didn't he come for us? For her? He said he'd return, but he left us in that tower, for Lord Khasar, for the knocking men, for the rats.

I must return to work. Tomorrow her khan is holding a feast for visiting gentry from Beloved of Ris, the realm to our northwest. We've been preparing for days and a mountain of pots teeter, waiting for the wash water.

I wonder, does he ever think of us? Does he remember? Has he snapped a pine needle just to smell it?

Day 71

It's past midnight and I've been just sitting here, staring at the fire. I don't want to write, but I may as well, since I can't sleep.

Tonight we scrubbed more pots than I thought existed in all the realms. As I was hauling water in from the well, Koke, one of the serving boys, brought us his apron and asked if we could wash a spill out of it. Qacha grabbed it. She thinks Koke's a sweet boy, and he thinks she's the prettiest thing since the first flower. I think he spilled brown sauce down his front as an excuse to approach her. Osol the cutter came over while we talked with Koke, and he smiled at me once. I smiled back. Why wouldn't I?

"You should see the lady," Koke said. "The clothes she's wearing have so much embroidery, there's not a lick of plain cloth left. Even so, she's not pretty, though she's not like—"

He glanced at me and I think he was sorry he'd said it. I didn't want him to feel sorry, he's a good boy mostly, so I asked, "Who is she?"

"Lady Vachir? She's the ruling lady from Beloved of Ris. It's for her Khan Tegus is having the feast, you know. What with Lord Khasar bringing war to his right and his left, Song for Evela needs all the other realms to be allies as close as family, and Beloved of Ris is our nearest neighbor, now that Titor's Garden is ashes. Everyone expected Khan Tegus and Lady Vachir would announce their betrothal tonight, and sure enough—"

I dropped the bucket. I splashed water over me, soaking my deel robe two hands up the hem and breaking the bucket's handle in the process. Qacha tried to fix it for me fast, before Cook noticed. Gal ran for another bucket to fetch more water. My lady and I just stood there.

They asked me what was wrong, if I felt faint, if I should sit down. Qacha sang me the song for sudden illness and stroked my hair. No one noticed my lady, how pale she looked, how her hand trembled. I noticed. I should have gone to her, I should have counseled with her, sung to her, combed her hair. But I couldn't move.

Later

I guess I thought we'd work in the kitchens until Saren came to her senses, until she shook off the terror, breathed free of the tower, and saw fit to be a lady again. I guess I thought he'd wait for her forever, never love another. What should I do? What can I?

Day 74

Lady Vachir is gone now. They'll be wed this winter.

Day 78

News has tumbled down into the kitchens. Lord Khasar overcame Goda's Second Gift. He did not raze it, as those traders had hoped. He killed all gentry and swore all the warriors who'd survived into his own army.

I watched Gal as she listened to news of her

homeland, but if her ears heard, her eyes didn't show it. I think she believes her family dead. I think she has less hope than a rock has sugar.

Koke said Khasar will most likely rest his warriors, train his new recruits, and then turn his eye to Song for Evela.

"Engaged to Lady Vachir in the nick of time," said Qacha. "Now the khan's warriors will unite with hers."

"Could Khasar come to Song for Evela?" I asked Koke.

"I'd bet a mare on it. He'll be here before winter, that's my guess."

I think about taking my lady away, but where would we run? Without a gher in winter, we'd die as fast as the honeybees. Cold is its own kind of tower.

Day 79

That boy Osol who winked at me, I saw him today winking at one of the cutter girls. I guess he's just a boy who winks. It doesn't matter, not in the least. And I'm not going to think about him anymore.

Day 80

It's not as though I would've married Osol.

Day 82

Last night I saw Qacha staring at her hands—split fingers, raw skin torn from washing. Scrubber work is hard on the hands.

"My mama was pretty at my age," she said.

Then this morning, Cook saw Qacha rubbing mare's milk butter all over her fingers. There was screaming and cursing, and when it all died down, Gal and I found Qacha sitting on the ground outside the kitchen, weeping and too afraid to enter. I'd never seen her cry before. Her face showed a welt the shape of a wooden spoon.

"Cook says she'll have my hair torn out if I come back in. But my papa can't keep me in the stables and I've nowhere to go. If I leave the city, I'd have to leave Papa, and Koke . . . how'll I ever see Koke again?"

I could've sung her a song of comfort, but that wouldn't cure the cause of the sobbing. I guessed she'd hoped the butter would keep her hands pretty. Someone once said I had beautiful hands.

"Gal, come with me a minute, will you?" I said. "Qacha, I'm going to go see if we can't get Cook in a good mood before you ask for your post back."

Cook was sweating over a pot, greasy black smoke rushing at her face.

I said, "We're caught up on all the pots and—oh, Cook, you look hot as a fire stone. Would you let Gal stir for you a moment while you sit a step back from the heat?"

"For a moment," Cook said, though she looked suspicious.

I sat her down, brought a stool for her feet, and begged a chance to rub her shoulders. While she rested, I hummed.

What ails Cook? I wondered, humming, touching her shoulders, trying to get a sense of her pain. Soon my hum turned into a song. I started out singing the song for body aches, for tiredness that runs over all of you like water over stones, the one that begins, "Tell me again, how does it go?" I could feel Cook want to get up and I thought I'd lost her, but then I guess she chose to let herself feel better for a time. Her shoulders relaxed beneath my hands.

Taking the tune for body aches, I wove in the words

for common pain, "Swan on her nest and the sunlight just so," while touching her shoulders, her back. I guessed her feet were sore, too, but I didn't dare touch them or she might figure out what I was up to. Her face was singed from smoke heat, her hands raw around calluses, and I closed my eyes and thought of the sound of the song going into those areas. She sighed, and I knew she was allowing the song to sink in. But there's usually something deeper than simple pain.

I tried weaving in a new song, the one for heartache that goes, "Tilly tilly, nar a black bird, nilly nilly, there a blue bird." I sang it softly, like you should when the hurt's buried deep and you want to ease it out slowly. It was just a guess, but who in all the realms doesn't have some heartache? Her shoulders tightened, then relaxed. I thought to go deeper.

"Prick, prick, blood on the cloth," I sang, now joining the song for body aches with the one for betrayal. No sooner had I begun than Cook lowered her head and sighed, long and sad as a wind stuck in a chimney. Suddenly, that large woman seemed as small and fragile as any tiny girl.

"Enough, I need to get back to work," said Cook, pushing me off and standing, but now her voice had lost its hard edge.

I rushed back to Qacha and told her now was

a good time to apologize. When she asked to be a scrubber again, Cook scolded her right proper, but there wasn't fire behind it. Within an hour, Qacha was scraping pots beside us.

"I've never seen Cook so calm," she said, already laughing again.

Gal asked, "Do you muckers have the changing powers like the desert shamans? Trick things into being what they're not?"

Qacha and I laughed. It was an absurd idea.

"Just the opposite," Qacha said. "The songs nudge things to be what they really are—a healthy body, a heart as calm as a baby's in the womb."

I agreed. "But there's no power in them, they're just songs."

"Well, I don't know about that, Dashti," said Qacha. "I could hear you singing back there, and I've never known someone to combine two songs together. That was clever. And choosing the right songs just for Cook—it's quite a feat to tame a beast like her."

"Cook did it, I just helped," I said.

My lady sidled up close to me, asking for a hand with a pot she couldn't get clean, and we all set in to work as hard as silence permits. A bit later, I noticed that Gal kept sneaking peeks at me, her face thoughtful.

Later that night in the dark by our hearth, I'd just dropped off to sleep, my head on Qacha's leg, when something poked me. When I opened my eyes to darkness, I gasped, for a moment terrified that the whole world was gone, that I was trapped in the tower again. But it was just night, just Gal prodding me awake. I eased away from Saren, lifting her arm from mine so she wouldn't wake, and sat up.

"I hear you humming at me sometimes," Gal said. "I run away from it because I haven't wanted to be anything but sad. But . . ." Gal's chin trembled, and she rubbed viciously at her face with the backs of her hands.

"Easy, Gal."

"I just don't know," her voice was a grating whisper, "don't know if my family's dead, don't know if they'll ever come for me. . . ."

"And you can't let yourself give up hoping," I said, "not until you're sure either way."

"But the hoping, that's what really hurts."

I reached for her and she shoved me off, then just as suddenly changed her mind and leaned into me, as if she'd never been hugged in her life and didn't know how to hug back.

I rocked her as we sat there, in the greasy dark of

157

the kitchen, snores bumping around us. I sang the song for bitter sorrow, "Darker river, blacker river, faster river, pulling me." She cried, softly at first, then harder, and then calmed, her head resting on my lap. She's sleeping like a newborn now.

It's funny, I don't feel tired at all. So I sit here and wish and wish that I could find the song that would heal my own lady.

Day 88

I'm hiding in the cheese closet and hating the close walls and dim light, and if Cook finds me I'll be out on my hide, but I must write this. Shria, the white-haired woman who first gave us work in the khan's house, came into the kitchens today. She said the khan had requested a mucker who knew the healing songs to attend to him, and Cook said, "Qacha, you're a mucker, aren't you?"

"Yes, but so's Dashti, and she's a better singer than I am, by leagues."

"Dashti would be best," said Gal, acting bold and pushing me right up to Shria. And she smiled like I didn't know she could. In the way that the sun's so bright in the city after the rain wipes the smoke from the air, that was Gal's face after crying all night. "Whatever ails the khan, Dashti will fix him right."

I stammered and looked at my lady, who offered no help.

And so Shria will come for me tomorrow. She'll take me to my lady's khan. I don't know what to think. I cannot think.

Day 89

All morning, my heart never let me forget what was to come. *Thump-thump, thump-thump,* it tapped at me. I didn't know when Shria would appear, so I stayed startled and alert all day. It reminded me of summers as a child before my brothers left, when our family set up our gher in the summer pastures and there were loads of children around. The Hunt, we'd play, some of us being animals hiding in the tall grass, the others searching us out with small bows and blunt arrows. How my heart would pound! I waited, crouched, prayed to Carthen, goddess of strength, and wanted to cry for the thrill and the terror. That's how I felt today.

I was up to my shoulders scrubbing a pot when white-haired Shria was suddenly before me.

"You're the mucker girl?"

Thank the Ancestors that I didn't actually scream, though the sound felt as real in my mouth as a bite of potato.

"Come with me, but wash first. You smell like grease and smoke."

She watched me as I scrubbed my arms and face, as if to make sure I did it properly. I asked to bring Saren with me. My thought was if her khan saw her, he'd sweep her back into his love and the life of gentry, and all would be put to right. But Shria didn't even bother to say no as she walked away. I pled with my lady not to scream and to let Qacha take care of her, then I ran after the woman.

Shria led me down a lush corridor, through two chambers, and into a small, dark room with a low ceiling like that in a gher. My lady's khan sat cross-legged on the floor, leaning forward to speak with two other men, and Shria and I stood quietly, waiting to be acknowledged. I was glad she was there. I've spent so long alone with Saren, I'd nearly forgotten that on entering the presence of gentry, I must keep quiet until he acknowledged me, or until I died, whichever came first. Just then, I was relieved to stand still. My feet were wood planks, my back a brick wall. My heart was so loud in

160

thumping I waited for Shria to scowl at me for being noisy.

You're a mucker, I reminded myself. You're not pretending to be Lady Saren and you're not trapped in a tower. You're just a mucker and a scrubber. You can be who you are just fine.

After a time, I found it interesting to watch her khan like that, my eyes free to rove over him. I could understand why my lady chose him. He must've been a fine boy, lean and strong, and now he had the bearing of a warrior. He also looked intelligent. Or at least there was humor in his eyes, which to my mind makes a person wiser. And I already know he can laugh.

Finally her khan looked up. Right at me. I think I might've gasped.

"Shria, is this the mucker girl? What's your name?"

"Dashti, my lord," I said, wondering if he'd ever known the name of Lady Saren's maid, but his eyes showed no recognition.

He dismissed Shria and sat on a low couch, continuing to address the two men. "Years ago, I met a mucker from Titor's Garden. She sang to me a healing song, made this old pain in my leg dissolve."

"If I'm not mistaken, my khan," said one of the men, "that's the injury I myself gave you."

"It was you, wasn't it, Batu?" Her khan's frown

161

twitched with humor. "I'd forgotten. You were teaching that slicing maneuver with your sword and I turned my horse the wrong way."

He straightened out on the couch, and I knelt beside him, placing my hands on his leg just below his knee where I thought I could feel the subtle heat that hovers around pain. He nodded at me once as if to say that I had my hands on the right spot, then continued to converse with the men.

I didn't dare sing for him the same songs I had in the tower. If he realized who I was, that I'd given him my shirt, I think I would just crumble like old bread underfoot. Instead I offered the song for new wounds. It's a battle song, urgent, fiery, "Hold, hold, strike and flee." Though he was absorbed in his conversation, I could tell it wasn't working. He seemed disappointed, the unease of his pain making him tired of the whole world.

So I took the risk and voiced the same songs from the tower, going up with "High, high, a bird on a cloud," and then down with, "Tell her a secret that makes her sigh." I watched his face—his eyes closed briefly, his forehead relaxed, his lips let out a long breath. But no remembrance of me.

I've spent these years wondering if he held my shirt to his face, if he knew my scent, if he'd recognize the smell of my skin like a mother cat knows her own kits. But not even the sound of my singing made him blink.

Day 91

It's been two days since I sat on her khan's floor, my hands on his leg. Shria said she'd come again if the khan requested me. I don't sleep well at night for wondering what I should do. I hear my lady snoring. She's sleeping on the kitchen floor, still in her dirty apron because she was too tired from scrubbing all day to take it off. I'm surely the worst lady's maid who ever lived under the Eternal Blue Sky.

Her khan is betrothed. There's a promise between him and Lady Vachir now. By rights, his betrothed can take the life of anyone who threatens her marriage. Even on the steppes, betrothal is sacred, and a man who carries off a betrothed girl is declared by all clans to be marked for slaying. I can't risk my lady's life by telling him she's here.

Then again, he and my lady were promised together first. Or were they? I mean, they promised their hearts to each other, but there couldn't have been a betrothal ceremony with ribbons of scarlet and brooms sweeping away the past. Her father never consented. If Lady Vachir asked for my lady's life, the chiefs of the city might find justice in her claim and grant it.

Besides, how would her khan be sure she really was his lady love? Will he remember her by sight? He hasn't seen her in at least four years. She must've been a girl when they met, and now she's a woman.

I'll have Qacha sing me the song for a clear head and think on this tomorrow.

Day 92

I've decided. I can't tell him yet. I need to be sure first that he'd welcome her, that there'd been a promise between them that would protect her from Lady Vachir.

"Was there a promise?" I asked my lady.

She was scrubbing a rag but going about it all wrong, just sort of massaging it with her fingers instead of rubbing it hard against itself. I took the rag from her and began to work at the stain until she snatched it back.

"I'll do it myself, Dashti. And I don't know what you mean about the promise. I don't remember."

Too often my lady talks this way. She says she

doesn't know anything and remembers less, and spends each hour in silence, scrubbing, scrubbing, scrubbing. I don't know why I bother to keep singing her the healing songs. Maybe there's nothing to heal.

Day 100

I've returned three times to her khan. Each time I sing to his pain and help his bones and muscles remember how they used to be whole. Sometimes the khan's chiefs sit in the room, talking low about war and Lord Khasar. Sometimes we're alone but for a guard outside the door, and the room is stuffed with silence. He hasn't spoken to me since the first day when he asked my name.

Day 103

Ancestors, I did speak when I should've been silent, I did forget who I was.

This afternoon, Shria returned me to the khan's low-ceilinged room and left me there. Khan Tegus was reading papers, and for many long minutes, perhaps an hour, I stood by the door. How my feet itched! But it felt like a solemn time, too, watching him read, seeing how he hunched his neck when the news was bad, how his cheek twitched with the idea of a smile when something amused him. He scratched his brow, his chin (and once, his rear end).

The looking reminded me of how I used to stare at the Sacred Mountain after Mama died. For hours I would gaze at the peak, imagining her soul making the journey up its slopes and back down to find the whole world transformed into the Ancestors' Realm, brimming with souls and dancing with light. I think sometimes just being silent and watching can change a person.

I draw this from memory, so it won't be right:

After some time he stretched, turned, and looked on me, looking for the time of a breath in and a breath out before his eyes focused and he realized he was staring at someone. He gasped.

"Lord Under but you startled me," he said. "I didn't realize anyone was here."

I laughed. I couldn't help it. He didn't seem to mind.

I set to work on his leg and I could sense the pain lifting from him fast. When I sang the pain out of his leg two weeks ago, it had taken much longer, finally easing in the time it takes water to boil over a fire. The more I work his leg, the better it remembers what it felt like to be whole and uninjured. In time, I guess his leg will heal itself entirely. And he won't need me.

Maybe that thought was what itched me to look deeper for another pain. I placed my hands on his belly, then his chest. His eyes opened. I could feel a heat inside him, a sharp heat, a yellow heat that comes from two broken bits of something rubbing against each other. Not an injury of flesh, but a hurt he refused to let go. This surprised me because in all my life, I've only been able to feel the heat pain like this with my own mama and with my lady, and once with a lamb I loved like a baby. And yet I could feel it so clearly in her khan.

"May I . . . may I sing to you again, my lord?" I asked.

"My leg feels fine. That will be all."

That will be all, he'd said, and that meant I should've left as quick as a fish. But how could I sense such a wound and not try to heal it? A bit of my mama awakened in me, a bit of the stubborn mucker soul, the stuff that keeps you alive when all the world is frozen and the food sacks empty. Any fool would be happy to die then and go to the Realm of the Ancestors, but only a mucker is stubborn enough to keep living.

"Sit down," I said.

I squeeze my eyes shut even as I write these words, though they're true. I did tell my lady's khan, the lord of Song for Evela, an honored gentry, to sit down. Forgive me, Nibus, god of order.

I kept my hands on his chest, and I could feel how strong he was. It reminded me of touching the neck of a horse as it runs, all those muscles under skin. Khan Tegus was a warrior, he could've knocked me to the roof and back down again. Instead he leaned back.

And I sang. "Berries in summer, red, purple, green." And I sang, "Digging and scratching, the earth bears a kin."

He leaned back more, he tensed and relaxed, the

muscles of his forehead tightened. Then all of a sudden he gasped, not in pain but surprise, and his arm flailed, scattering papers.

"Are you all right?" I asked. My hands took to shaking, and I patted him all over his chest and belly, making sure I hadn't hurt him.

His eyes were wide, but he nodded. "You pricked me just then. I can't explain it."

"Was it . . ." I hesitated. I didn't want to tell him his own feelings, but I thought I understood. "Was it as though you had a splinter inside, deep in your chest, that had been there so long you'd forgotten to notice the pain, and the song reminded you so you could pluck it out?"

I think he really saw me then for the first time, if that makes sense. He looked in my eyes, and he smiled and said, "Thank you, Dashti."

I hadn't known that he remembered my name. I can't say why, but his words made me want to cry, so I turned my head away and started gathering up the papers that had scattered. I felt him kneel beside me, heard the rustle of parchment as he picked up others.

"Where's that food storage account?" he mumbled after a time.

"Here, my lord," I said, handing him a paper.

"You read?"

"Yes, my lord, and write."

"And where do you work when you're not attending to me?"

"In the kitchens. I'm a scrubber."

"You read and write, you have the voice of the goddess Evela, and you scrub in the kitchens."

I laughed. "Evela's voice! I'm no pretty singer, no sit-and-listen singer. My mama used to say my singing voice is as rough as a cat's tongue and that's why my healing songs work. They dig at you, get inside, clean you up."

"Where's your mother now?"

"In the Realm of the Ancestors." And just like that I started to cry. Five years she's been gone. I should think I'd be used to it, but just saying those words to Khan Tegus was like being swatted in the face with the sadness all over again—maybe because for the first time I was telling him some of my own truth. I handed him the papers right quick and begged dismissal, walking out his door before he'd even given me leave.

When I think on all the times I sinned against her khan's nobility, I'm shocked I haven't been struck dead. Perhaps in the morning I'll wake as a pile of ash.

Day 104

Not ash yet.

Day 105

I'm writing this from a clean room with its own hearth, a horsehair blanket, and a wood table and chair. There's a window that looks over the dairy. The room's half the size of a gher and for now it's my own. How mama would laugh! Privacy's a strange notion to a mucker, where five in a tent is a roomy place.

Yesterday Shria told Cook, "Dashti will be living upstairs so she can copy notes for the chiefs and attend to Khan Tegus with the healing songs."

Saren didn't like it, but what could I do? I begged Qacha to look out for her and help her keep up with her scrubbing, said good-bye, and that quickly, here I am. Perhaps I should've found a way to stay with my lady, but she's improved very little since the tower, and my daily singing doesn't heal her a bit. Maybe it won't hurt either of us to be apart.

I've spent the past two days brushing ink on paper, making copies of lists about supplies and weapons, and looking out the window to ease the cramping in my eyeballs.

Windows are the eyes of the Ancestors. Windows are better than food!

I had a free hour this morning and went back to the kitchens to fetch this book from where I'd hidden it beneath some empty grain sacks. No one in the kitchens can read, so far as I know, but I'd rather not risk it being found. There are things written in here that could get me hanged on the south wall.

The girls cheered to see me and wanted all the details, so I washed pots and described my room and the window and the horsehair blanket. My lady didn't speak a word. She wouldn't even meet my eyes. Sometimes I have to snap a twig to keep from shouting, "Why don't you tell him who you are? Why don't you smile? Why don't you stop worrying about your father and Khasar and the tower and just decide to be Lady Saren?"

I should scratch out those words. Maybe later.

Day 109

Lately all I do is write. I copy pages of notes, lists of food supplies, numbers of weapons. As I fall asleep, the soft sound of a brush grazing parchment continues to murmur in my ear. Already my scrubber hands have begun to heal and my ink stains make me feel like a real scribe. I'm mostly alone, but white-haired Shria comes to take the papers to the khan's chiefs, and twice a day Qacha brings my meals from the kitchen.

Sometimes when I'm sitting on the floor eating with Qacha, I feel about as content as a bird with a good lifting wind. In greeting, we always clasp forearms, touch cheeks, and inhale through our noses so as to breathe in each other's scent. Smell is the voice of the soul, and this greeting is the most intimate. It's common among family and clan, of course, but I've been on my own for so long, I'd forgotten how warm and wonderful it is.

And whenever I can, I return to the kitchen to see my lady and the other girls or walk around the stables and dairy and soak in the cheery summer sun. The window is wonderful, but any walls remind me of the tower.

I haven't seen her khan since I came to this small, clean room.

Day 111

Shria called me to the khan's chamber today. I was startled to see it full, seven of the khan's chiefs present, several shamans, all arguing about Khasar and scouting reports and the state of the city with the refugees near bursting the walls. Three other scribes were there. I joined them by the wall, taking notes of the talk as quickly as I could.

Khan Tegus never looked at me. I'm a mucker maid. I guess I needed to be reminded of that. So, good. Fine. Sometimes my fancy gets to floating inside me, threatening to carry me away like a leaf on a wind. Better to be a stone.

Day 112

Shria came flustering for me this morning.

"Come! Quick!"

We raced down the corridors, up another flight of stairs, and into the last of the khan's chain of rooms.

174

The first thing I noticed was a man lying on the floor and bleeding, bleeding fast. Another man was in the corner, his ankles and wrists tied with sashes, animal scratches on his face. Three men with drawn swords were guarding the bound man, all tense as a gher roof, shaking slightly as if hoping for a reason to stab the bound man through. I stopped on the threshold. I wobbled.

"Here's the mucker girl, my lord," said Shria.

The khan pulled me toward the wounded man. "My friend is hurt. Sing for him."

"I . . . I can't, my lord. A healing song can't stop blood from flowing or close a wound."

"Help him, Dashti."

How I longed for the voice of Evela and the strength of Carthen, for powers as mighty as the desert shamans are rumored to possess, for a way to force that man's body to do my will and heal itself. But I felt as thin as grass. I sat by the man's head, I touched his face. My body shook so hard I thought I heard my bones rattle, and I wondered if my limbs would fall right off.

Sing to him, Dashti, I ordered myself, but before I could find a tune, I got to thinking of Mama with the fever, her skin as yellow as this paper I write on, her lips dry like a snake shedding its skin. For hours, for days I sang to her. I pushed my soul into the words till my voice rasped to ashes. But she fell asleep, deeper and deeper till her skin went cold.

A shaman knelt beside me, letting his hands hover over the bleeding man's chest. Until I recognized his face, I didn't realize he was a shaman because he was dressed only in a robe and for some reason had removed his tassled hat and belt with nine mirrors.

"I feel a pulsing heat," said the shaman, his eyes closed. "The life heat leaves his body even as his blood does. His soul is teetering on a threshold, undecided to live or die."

"Help him to live," said Khan Tegus. He was speaking to me and to the shaman and he seemed near crying. "Tell his soul to live!"

Who am I to tell a man to live? Who am I to claim the powers of the Ancestors? I moved aside so the shaman could have more room to do his holy work. He's climbed the Sacred Mountain and seen the faces of the Ancestors. I have no place beside him.

I sat quietly in a corner, though I was tempted to curse like the horse wranglers and kick a chair. I was so angry at myself for not being smart enough, for not being a true healer, but I just sing the easing songs, the slow and cheery songs, the animal songs.

Later

When Qacha brought dinner to my room, she whispered that the bleeding man is an important chief to the khan.

"And the man who stabbed him?" I asked.

"An assassin. Sent by Lord Khasar to kill Khan Tegus, or so Koke heard."

"What less should we expect from the lord of the realm named for Under, god of tricks?"

"True enough, but Under played a trick back on him today. A shaman was present, and when the assassin attacked, I hear the shaman took fox form and leaped between the khan and the assassin. It seems not even Lord Khasar's warrior would dare to harm a fox."

"Ah," I said, the animal scratches on the assassin's face making sense, and the shaman wearing just his robe. He must've lost his clothes when he changed. Would that I'd been there to see that!

So it seems Under played everyone today. The khan is unharmed, but the assassin's blade still found a true mark. He's a slippery one, that Under. I knelt to the north and prayed thanks that Khan Tegus was protected, but I don't much like depending on the god of tricks.

Day 113

Morning was still as dark as night when someone tapped at my door. I wrapped my wool robe over my sleep clothes, thinking it must be Shria with an errand. Instead I found my lady's khan.

He looked as tired as dawn, and he leaned against my door and just stared at me for a time, eyes half closed. I hadn't realized that I'd stopped breathing until I heard him breathe in deeply. He said, "I know you'll say it's hopeless, that you won't be able to help, but Dashti, will you come with me?"

I didn't ask what he meant as I followed him down the dark corridor. I'd been too startled to think of putting on shoes, and the floor was slippery with cold. The blind walls around us reminded me of the tower, and I spent the walk imagining what those three years would've been like if my companion in the dark had been someone else.

We entered his chambers and the air was thick with the sweet smoke of burning juniper. A shaman woman was doing her wild dance between the bed and the fire, beating a flat drum, the tassels on her hat flying.

"You may rest for a moment, holy one," 'said Khan Tegus, and the woman stopped spinning and sat in the corner. For a moment, I could see my own face reflected in one of the nine mirrors on her belt. I looked away.

The bleeding man was asleep on a low couch, his chest rising and falling too fast for sleep. Khan Tegus knelt by the bed. I knelt beside him.

"The shamans tell me they've done what they can, but there's no change," said Khan Tegus. "They tell me that when all that blood poured out of Batu, his soul flowed with it. Now it's dislodged from his breast and wavering on the edge of his body."

The man's face was pale. I touched his arm and found the skin was prickly hot. "His soul doesn't know whether to stay or go."

The khan met my eyes straight on. He didn't blink as he said, "Help it to stay."

I looked at the shaman, squatting by the fire and humming. I knew to complete her training, she must've climbed the Sacred Mountain, fasted from all food, and prayed for four days, naked under the sky. Bareness is the ultimate debasement, so that's why shamans do it, to submit themselves completely to the

Ancestors, and even more, to prostrate themselves under the Eternal Blue Sky, naked and new as a baby.

These shaman healers had their souls washed by the Eternal Blue Sky. Who was I to try where they had failed?

"My lord—," I started.

"Please." The khan rubbed his eyes so I couldn't see his face, but I could hear how his voice was worn to crumbling. "Batu is my friend, but he's also my chief of war. Khasar is on the move, set to tear out the throat of my army, and I can't lose anyone else. Please help him, Dashti."

Right then, I would've scaled the forbidden heights of the Sacred Mountain for him, but I didn't know how to do what he asked.

The healing songs help things be as they are at first, as they want to be again. I wondered, could I sing to the man's very soul? Help it return to his breast and sleep peacefully again? If there's a song for souls, my mama never taught it.

I wanted to run away, I felt so useless and ashamed! But I couldn't. Khan Tegus had given me a pine bough and My Lord the cat, he let me sing the pain out of him, he remembered my name. I had to try.

I took Batu's hand, closed my eyes so my whole world was touch and sound, said a silent prayer to

Evela, goddess of sunlight and songs, and began to sing. I didn't know what song would come out of my mouth until I heard it.

"Little bird, little bird, that twits and flits and flies. Little bird, little bird, unfold your feathered skies."

It's not a healing song, it's a play song, one the mucker children sing in the spring, racing in a circle, leaping over stones. I almost laughed to hear myself sing it. I don't know why that song felt right. Maybe because it makes such a happy noise; the tune likes to skip on my tongue and tickle my throat.

The shaman glared at me through the tassels on her hat, as though saying, *That's not a reverent song for the dying!* I glared back, as though saying, *The whole point is to stop the dying!* I think Khan Tegus must've noticed the abundance of glares, for after a minute he dismissed the shaman from the room. We were alone now. I kept singing.

Sing to his soul, I told myself. So I sang more happy songs, things to remind him of how rich is living, how blue is the Eternal Sky, how good roasted meat tastes with a sprinkling of salt, how the steppes fill with thousands of yellow heartsong flowers after the frost breaks. When I began the lighthearted song that goes, "Bread on the stones, Mama, and how the belly groans," her khan joined in, knowing that one

181

from his own childhood, I guess. Beneath my own voice, his felt like a horsehair blanket, rough and warm.

After a time, I let her khan sing that one alone, while I wove in "the earth breathes, the earth sings, its soul moves in the rivers," and other healing songs for sickness and injury.

Batu's breathing slowed, his voice mumbled sleepily in his throat, and if I were smart enough to know such things, I'd say his soul slipped back inside, curled up like a cat in his chest, and purred to be home.

By then, her khan was sitting on the floor beside me. He leaned his back against the couch, stretching his legs out before him. I leaned back, too. We both knew Batu was better. We didn't have to say it.

"You may return to your room, if you wish," he said.

I shrugged. "I won't sleep any more tonight."

"Neither will I." He watched the flames in the hearth. "It's a wondrous gift you have. I can't help wonder how muckers know songs that shamans have never heard."

I sighed before I talked, just because it felt right. "The people of stone walls, the ones who live in cities, they have healers to call and shamans to bless them. But the people of the felt walls, alone with the

182

wind and grass, would die if Evela, goddess of sun-light, hadn't taken pity on us. She gave muckers the healing songs to help us keep living beneath her sun-shine. Or so my mama said. And I believe her. You'd be a fool to doubt her. The grasses themselves bowed down before her foot touched them."

He chuckled, and when I asked him why, he said he'd had such a mother, too. She'd gone to the Ancestors' Realm seven years ago, but was such a powerful presence he still thinks to check that his sash is tied straight each morning so she won't scold him.

"And she named you Tegus," I muttered.

"What was that?"

"I was just thinking," I said, "how you can tell something about a woman by what she names her chil-dren. Tegus means *perfect* in the naming language."

He made a face. "I haven't always relished that name. My cousins gave me much grief about it grow-ing up."

"I think it's lovely. I mean . . ." I returned my gaze to the fire, because it was easier to talk to him that way. "What I mean to say is, it's lovely to think of your mother holding her first baby, and looking at your fingers and toes, your eyes, your lips, and say-ing, 'Perfect. He's perfect. My Tegus.'"

"I can imagine her saying those very words." He was quiet a moment. "Dashti. That means 'one who is good luck,' doesn't it?"

"Another name that caused teasing. It's not an easy thing to wear a mark of bad luck on my face and have a name that means good luck. The story goes that a clan sister helped with my birth, and when she saw me, she told my mother, 'She should be called Alagh,' meaning *mottled*, you know. My father saw me and said, 'You must call her Alagh so all know she is destined for bad luck.' So my mama said, 'Her name is Dashti.'"

He raised his bowl of milk tea. "Let's drink to stubborn mothers."

He took a long sip, then offered the bowl to me. The same that he had drunk from. He shared a drink with me, gentry with commoner. I took it with both my hands to show my reverence, and when I drank, the warmth seemed to fill not just my belly, but my entire body down to my toes.

We kept watching the fire and talking about mothers and other things. I tried to keep in mind his status, but I was drowsy, and the sight of a fire sings its own kind of healing song, one that seems to say, "Easy, slow and easy, all is well." It reminded me of his third visit to the tower, when he sat on the ground and leaned against the wall, and I leaned on the other side, and we just talked. And the Ancestors let us.

He looked at my feet and said suddenly, "You're not wearing shoes."

I wiggled my toes. "I guess I'm not. But at least my sash is tied straight."

"Hmph, no comparison. What would your right good mucker mother say to that, walking around in bare feet?"

I had a joke on my lips about skinny ankles and had to choke it back. So near I came to revealing myself!

"What's wrong?" he asked, sitting up at my silence. "Are you hungry? Should I send for something?"

"No, strangely. Usually I could eat a plate of anything and be ready for another, but right now I don't want to eat." And I didn't. But mostly I didn't want him to get up and call for someone who might stay. Food wasn't worth losing our bit of peace.

He mumbled agreement and relaxed again, his back against the couch. Our shoulders almost touched. The heat between us mingled.

"May I ask you something, honored khan?"

"If you call me Tegus," he said. "You helped save Batu. You earned the right to say my name."

185

"Tegus," I said, and the name in my mouth tasted wonderful, so in my heart I quickly asked forgiveness from Nibus, god of order. "A few weeks ago, when I sang to your deep pain, what was it? What old hurt were you carrying?"

"Nothing I didn't deserve." His eyelids half closed and I thought he wouldn't answer, and rightly he shouldn't have—it was an impertinent question. But soon he went on. "I was in love with a lady once. I thought I didn't have the power to save her, so I didn't even try. And she came to harm because of my reluctance, my stupidity."

I didn't argue with him about the stupidity part, Ancestors forgive me. I did wonder, *Why didn't you come back for us? Back for her?* But I didn't dare ask her khan that, and I couldn't ask Tegus. The song of the fire's snaps seemed a bit sadder now, as though it realized it was dying and was sorry to go.

Behind us, Batu stirred in his sleep, and at the same time Tegus and I both placed a hand on the war chief's arm. Tegus smiled at me when he saw that my instinct to comfort had been the same as his, and he didn't withdraw. The moment made me imagine how her khan will be as a father, how he'll sit up at night and hold his wife's hand and talk to her as she rocks the baby to sleep.

Saren could only be happy with such a man.

He said he was in love with her. I am her maid. I must do what I can.

Day 115

Today I managed to get my half day free during Saren's time off. We walked through the streets where folk who escaped from Titor's Garden and Goda's Second Gift pitch tents and sleep on door-steps. Saren kept her arm in mine, leaning as if she needed the support, all that air and sky making her feel unsteady.

"I've spent some time with your khan, my lady, and I know he's a good man. He's safe." It was hard not to laugh outright as I added, "He's not plotting to kill you with arrows and knives."

She frowned but didn't argue, so I went on.

"I'm going to say something that you may not want to hear—being in the tower did you harm, made you believe things that just aren't real. I'm sorry it's so, but it's true."

"I know," she said, really quiet, but she still said it.

"So you need to trust me, my lady, when I tell you that Khan Tegus is safe. He'll take care of you.

He was very much in love with you, and still is, despite his engagement. Though it's been years, my lady, he remembers you with sighs."

"He does?" She breathed in as she asked it.

"Oh yes. He still remembers the words of your letters, and I think he holds the image of your face in his heart."

She seemed confused, or maybe she was just thinking. With my lady, both attitudes appear the same. But she wasn't arguing, which was more than I'd hoped for.

"He's engaged," I admitted, "and that's another matter. But if he still loves you, and he promised himself to you first, then Lady Vachir can have nothing to say. There is a risk, but how can we keep living in his very house and not let him know?"

She stopped walking. Her face was fully in the sun, and I noticed how pale she was, how little she must leave the kitchens, how she's still bricked up in the tower. Her eyes spoke it most of all—dull, never looking far ahead.

"But . . . but he didn't come back."

I had no answer for that. "I don't know why, but I do know his heart was broken, and you have the power to heal him. How can you not?"

"I can't just go to him, claiming to be Lady Saren."

"But you *are* Lady Saren."

She looked at her hands. The wash water had done its damage—fingertips splitting, palms callused and bruised, skin mottled red almost as dark as my own birthmarks. Didn't I once take an oath to keep her hands beautiful? My heart turned, and if we hadn't been standing in the street, I would've knelt before her and begged forgiveness. Instead, I took her worn hands and kissed each one.

"How I've failed you, my lady. I will help you. I'll do whatever you ask to set you back in your place again."

She wrinkled her brow, thinking hard for a few moments, then said, "Pretend to be me, Dashti. Say you're me. Find out what he'd do, how he'd react, and if it's favorable, then I'll tell all."

"My lady, it was one thing in the tower when he couldn't see my face—"

"He won't know me by sight."

"It's been years, I know, but still . . ." My face. My blotchy face and arm, my dull hair, my solid mucker body, my everything that isn't like my lady.

"You swore an oath," she said.

And so I had. Oath breakers will find no haven in the Ancestors' Realm where my mama waits. And besides, it's not fair to ask my lady to risk her life

189

against Lady Vachir's wrath. I am her maid. It should be my duty to keep her from harm and face it myself. But to pretend to be Lady Saren again, and this time not hidden in a dark tower but out under the Eternal Blue Sky. . . .

My stomach's icy cold, and I don't feel like writing anymore. I'll sketch instead.

Day 119

I wasted three days worrying, praying for the lie I hadn't yet made, and imagining Tegus's face when I spoke the false words "I'm Lady Saren." Three days wasted, and my lady remains a scrubber indefinitely, because now her khan is gone.

His warriors marched today, sudden, like when the wind shifts from west to south. They left as soon as word came from Beloved of Ris—Khasar's armies are advancing on that realm.

Everyone thought Khasar would attack Song for Evela next because he proclaimed he'd have Tegus's title of khan for himself. It seems he isn't coming for it yet, instead striking at the weaker realm first.

We may not hear news for days and weeks. I feel set to cry and kick and curse.

There's not as much scribe work now while the khan is absent, so I volunteered to go back to the kitchens. I don't mind leaving my little room so much. Privacy begins to feel somewhat like loneliness.

Day 122

No news of her khan. It's getting cold at night. I wonder if he has enough blankets.

Day 125

Still no news. I feel dog-crazy, as if I'd like to bite someone. This kitchen smells.

Day 126

Mama would scold me. All I seem to do is mope, mope, mope. No one has enough news for me. Osol set to winking at me again, but I'm all worry with no space left to sigh for a cutter boy. I wash rags as if I held Lord Khasar's neck in my hands. I scrub pots as though the faster they're clean the sooner the war will be done. Cook declared at the rate I was going I'd soon have her position. Then she laughed. Scrubber is the lowest position in the kitchens, of course.

"I'm a scribe," I said.

She laughed again.

And while I mope, my lady scowls.

"You swore an oath," she whispered at me while we scrubbed. "And then you didn't do it."

I washed my next pot a little harder.

Day 127

I can't believe . . . the news is too big to write, I can't make my letters large enough to contain what I have to say. But I must say it somehow.

He's alive! He's here, he's strong and pretty as ever he was, and purring like to shake the house down.

My Lord the cat, my beautiful cat.

He must've escaped the wolf, must've scratched that demon's eyes and run straight home. In the way he used to know when it was morning though the tower was all darkness, he must've known how to find the land of her khan again. Cats are wise like that. They have a shaman's eyes.

Today was my half day free, and I went to visit Mucker in the stable, only he was out pulling a cart. So I just wandered, because the sun was pleasant and round above me and made my shadow look strong and straight. I was thinking how you can't tell if a person's beautiful or not by her shadow when I saw a gray tail disappear into the dairy.

He was gone so quickly I couldn't be sure, so I ran after him, slipped on some spilled milk, and slid under the dairyman's legs. He hollered at me and before he could kick me out, I blurted, "Excuse me, but my cat came in here."

My Lord the cat leaped up on a stall, balancing above our heads.

"And how am I to know that he's yours?" the dairyman asked.

Khan Tegus gave him to me, I wanted to say, but of

course I couldn't. If I'd thought of a good lie, I would've spoken it just then and let the Ancestors strike me dumb, so desperately I wanted to hold My Lord again.

I'd started to stutter something when My Lord leaped down onto my shoulder and wrapped his tail around my neck, just as he used to do in the tower. The dairyman laughed.

"Looks like he's yours, right enough. Get him out of here, then."

He remembers me. Don't these letters I'm writing fairly dance off the page? He's alive, and he remembers me!

These past days, it seemed I could scarcely draw breath for feeling so gray, and then today . . . well, the change makes me think about the sky over the steppes, cloudy one moment and Eternal Blue Sky the next. There's never a day that we don't see some blue sky. That's the way with a mucker's emotions, too. My mama used to say, "Are you sad? Then just wait a minute."

Day 128

My Lord the cat slept beside me last night. I didn't wake up once.

Day 129

All the girls are utterly smitten with My Lord, of course. He sits on my shoulders, and they gather around and coo. Qacha can't help petting him whenever she passes by, even when her hands are sudsy. A wet coat puts My Lord in grumpy spirits, but he never shirks the attention. Cook complained about him at first, but soon she was saying things like, "That cat's prettier than a man," and "I'd eat my own toenails before I'd cook that one up."

Day 131

I love My Lord the cat! I love him, I love him. He sleeps again in the curve of my belly, he purrs when I wake in the night for wondering about the war and her khan and the lie I must tell. His rumbling song soothes me back to sleep. He is even better than windows.

Day 133

Last night as I lay down by the kitchen hearth, My Lord loped in from somewhere and took his place against my side. Snores already surrounded us. As I settled in, I noticed that my lady was awake, watching me. Watching us.

She whispered, "Why is he your cat? Didn't Khan Tegus give him to me?"

"Well, he gave him to me—"

"After you told him you were Lady Saren."

I didn't answer. My heart felt like a furnace spitting fire.

"I think he should be mine." She reached out and grabbed him from my arms and pulled him to her own side. He writhed free and came back. Again she grabbed him, and this time in the struggle he clawed her arm and made an angry "rawr!" that provoked Gal to snort in her sleep.

"I'm sorry, my lady," I said, though I wasn't. I liked very much that My Lord preferred me. I rather felt like clawing her myself.

I hadn't even realized until that moment how over these past weeks, I'd begun to bubble with dark things, and my heart was boiled hard like tough mutton. I don't think I've ever truly hated a thing in my life like I hated Saren then. Hated everything about her—the whine her voice took as though she thought herself a child of six, her perfect face and shiny black hair, her honored father, her smell, her shaking hands when she stood under the sky. Her cowardice, her slowness. Her everything. I hated her.

I curled back up with My Lord alongside my body and pretended to be asleep. After a time, I heard sniffling. There's nothing more aggravating in the world than the midnight sniffling of the person you've decided to hate.

Finally I sat up, and My Lord the cat, annoyed with all the talking and wiggling, sprang away to the door and set to cleaning his paws.

"What's wrong now, my lady?" I asked, and not very nicely.

She started to cry. Of course. "I order you to do one more thing for me."

She wants the cat, I thought. Let her try and take him.

"I want," she said, sniffling and sobbing, "I want you to kill me."

My lady never plays games with words. She means everything fully, she drinks down the world

197

whole and spits nothing out. I knew she meant what she said, and it set me spinning.

"No," I whispered, my throat dry as salt meat.

"I order you to—"

"Order until you're out of breath," I said, glancing at Gal and Qacha, who were still dead asleep. "If I did such a thing, there'd be no place for me in the Ancestors' Realm, nor for you either. We'd wander in the gray beyond the borders forever, with nowhere to sit and no milk to drink, and I'd never see my mama again. Punishment for disobeying your order can't be worse than that."

Saren turned on her side, her back to me, and set to sobbing so violently I thought she'd vomit.

"I don't want to live anymore," she said, the words almost lost with each wet sob. "Every night I think the sun's gone forever, but when it rises in the morning anyway I wish it wouldn't. Because then I spend all day scrubbing. And my chest hurts like it's stuffed with rocks. And everyone's dead in my father's city. Because of me. All those bodies, because of me. Because I wouldn't marry Khasar. It's my fault and it's too much and I can't carry it anymore. And Khasar's still coming for me anyway. He'll find the tower empty and come looking. And Khan Tegus will never love me because I'm not clever and I smell like dirty pots and I want to die, Dashti. Please, I can't do it myself, I've tried. I'm too afraid and I'll do it wrong. You have to do it for me. Please, Dashti."

I didn't move all the while she pleaded. I felt buried by her sobs and words.

I turned toward My Lord and very quietly sang the cat song, the slow, sliding song that goes, "Twitch and itch, the world is meat, the world is mine." He put his nose out as if he could smell the song, then he padded to me and pressed his head against mine. I felt a jab in my heart as though someone had just told me that he was dead after all and never coming home.

Then I sat behind my lady, sang the cat song, wrapped my arms around her shoulders, and placed the cat onto her lap.

"Now you sing," I said.

At first she was timid and still sobbing too hard for the cat to hear any tune, but she calmed and her voice found the song.

"Temple to tail, purr zipping through." Her voice was softer than mine, but sweeter too. Whereas my singing's a hot, hearty meal, hers is a drink of sugared milk.

I didn't know if My Lord would accept her song or if he'd scorn her still—it's always the hearer's choice to heed a calling song, and cats are more stubborn than most. But he is a friendly cat, a happy soul. He curled up inside her crossed legs. After a time, he purred. She's no mucker, but that song she sang as well as my own mama.

She kept on singing and stroked his fur, but she stayed rigidly still as if afraid to spook him.

"It's all right. You can lie down," I said. "I think he'll stay with you."

Very slowly, very carefully, she eased herself down on her side. My Lord curled up beside her with a pleased rumble.

It was a long time before I slept that night, and I slept fitfully. When I sat up again, the fire was lower, and everyone was still snoozing except for Saren, who kept whisper-singing all night long and stroking his fur. My Lord the cat lay asleep, nestled in the curve of her body.

Except for singing my mama into the Ancestors' Realm, giving My Lord to Saren was the hardest thing I've ever done. And I felt emptied, a well dug out of my chest, and as pathetic as a three-legged cricket. But, strangely, as I rolled over to find sleep again, I realized that I didn't hate her anymore.

Day 134

When My Lord the cat came in from his morning prowl, Saren sang the song for cats, and he jumped onto her shoulder, curling his tail around her neck.

Qacha touched my elbow. "Dashti, Sar is—"

"I know," I said. It's a gross sin among muckers to sing a calling song to another person's animal, so I explained, "I gave her permission. He's her cat now. He was all along, actually. I was the one who first took him from her."

Qacha shook her head as though she didn't believe me. She doesn't think so highly of Saren. Not knowing that she's an honored lady, how can she be expected to be patient with this girl who doesn't do her share of work, who won't talk to anyone but me, who fusses like a small child when I'm not around? I understand Qacha's glares, but then I see Saren smiling at the cat as he extends his nose to hers, and my heart does a little flip. A happy flip, I think.

Still no news from her khan's army.

Day 136

Something has happened, and I thought I needed to write it down so my nerves can quiet, but now I hesitate. There was a tribunal today and . . . Ancestors, how my stomach hurts! Let me distract myself with other thoughts first.

I never realized before that every city in the Eight Realms has eight chiefs as well as a lord or lady—nine rulers to mirror the sacred nine, the eight Ancestors plus the Eternal Blue Sky. Each chief serves one of the Ancestors and is always of the opposite gender. For instance, Batu, the war chief, serves Carthen, goddess of strength. I like to see things ordered, and right now I need a bit of calming, so I'll jot it down here:

Khan Tegus (lord of the city)—serves the Eternal Blue Sky, and so is over all.

Chief of war (commands the warriors)—serves Carthen, goddess of strength.

Chief of city (maintains walls, structures, and trade routes)—serves Ris, god of roads and towns.

Chief of animals (keeps livestock, dairies, monitors hunting in the woods)—serves Titor, god of animals.

Chief of food (supervises the farms that feed the city and the market, and keeps the town's food supply)—serves Vera, goddess of farms and food.

Chief of order (sits in judgment)—serves Nibus, god of order.

Chief of night (leads the night watch, keeps the peace)—serves Goda, goddess of sleep.

Chief of light (hosts festivals and directs the shamans)—serves Evela, goddess of sunlight.

Once I learned all this, I wanted to know, what about the eighth chief? The one who would serve Under, god of tricks? Koke explained that she's the invisible chief, and there's always an empty chair for her at counsels. That thought scattered skin prickles down my back.

So I'm going to record now what's happened, though my stomach squeezes just to think of it. But it pesters my mind, so I will. The tribunal today was for Osol, the boy who used to wink at me, who once gave me a wildflower. Word in the kitchens is that he and a girl were having loud words in the dairy, and the chief of animals was passing through. When she heard the ruckus, she commanded them to silence, but Osol was in a rage and pushed the chief, and when she fell, he kicked her.

For minor offenses, the chief of order would

decide punishment, but this is not minor. The chief of animals is one of the khan's cousins, so she's gentry. Without Khan Tegus and Batu, there are still six chiefs in the city (plus the empty chair), and it only takes four of the nine to pass judgment. So they met together and they decided—Osol will hang tonight on the south wall.

I know this is the punishment for such an offense. I know I shouldn't be stunned, but I never knew a person who was hanged. I've glimpsed the bodies sometimes, hanging there, but I never knew. It changes it all. It makes me cry to miss seeing his smile, it makes me wince at the memory of his winking, it makes me shudder to imagine how he's feeling tonight. It makes me feel as if I'm the one who will hang.

He shouldn't have struck gentry, no, but Ancestors, does he really deserve death? Sometimes I wonder if that eighth chief, the absent one who serves Under, isn't getting more of a voice in things than we suspect.

Day 137

Osol died last night. I won't go see his body.

Day 140

I haven't had time to pick up the brush and ink these past days because I've been working my fingers to the marrow, but here's my news—so has my lady! She scrubs and mops and hauls water, and she hums all the while. And when Cook says, "Hurry with that pot, girl," my lady smiles, dimples and all. Under strike me silly if I lie.

She has her willow tree moments, she has her mopes, and she still startles at sudden sounds like a dropped pot or slammed door. But other times, in the in-between easy moments, she's calmer than pond water. Sometimes, she even seems happy.

I keep kissing her cheek and once I tickled her side, and hear this—she laughed! She says such things as, "Look at how clean that rag is," and "That's a pot I'd eat out of, sure enough." After she worked through her stack of pots today, Cook let her take over the stirring of the soup kettle, and I thought Saren would burst from joy. It's that cat's doing, no doubt in me. The creature loves her true as true, and she knows it. It's the knowing that's made the difference, I think. He wraps around her ankles or neck, even when she isn't singing to him. He finds her at night and purrs into her belly. A cat can make you feel well rested when you're tired or turn a rage into a calm just by sitting on your lap. His very nearness is a healing song.

We've all been worked to bruising lately because now we cook for Lady Vachir and a large entourage from Beloved of Ris. They fled the war and a feared winter siege. I wish they'd brought more news with them. So far, I've learned little about our khan's warriors and how they fare, but surely the Ancestors will protect them.

When her khan returns, I don't rightly know how I'll tell him I'm Lady Saren. Having his current betrothed sleeping in his house does add a complication to this already thorny situation. Thank the Ancestors I hadn't made the claim before. With Khan Tegus gone, there'd be no one to prevent Lady Vachir from deeming me a threat to her betrothal and taking my life. That's how the law's written, that's how Nibus, god of order, made the world. And Osol's death has reminded me that the chiefs wouldn't hesitate to carry out that law.

Day 145

Last week, Cook was so impressed with my lady's new devotion to working, she moved Saren out of the scrubbing kitchen and into the presenting kitchen, where she arranges food on the platters before they're taken up. It's one step below server and one of the highest duties any kitchen worker achieves. Saren fairly glowed at the news. My Lord entwines himself in her ankles, and she hums as she works, her cheeks bright and pink as though she were a healthy mucker girl living under the sun.

"Cook only chose her because she's pretty," said Gal, "in case she moves up to server. It's not fair. You're the fastest worker in the kitchens. It should've been you."

"It doesn't matter. I'm a scribe," I said, though I don't know if I'll ever be again.

Today was my free half day, and I sprang outdoors and into the city. I was anxious to see if I could find any news about the khan's army, but all the talk was the same—Khasar invincible, bloodshed imminent—enough dismay and fear to please Under, god of tricks, for years to come.

I passed the jobbers market where refugees stand in long rows hoping for employment, all holding the symbols of their trade: jewelers with magnifying glasses, goldsmiths with tiny mallets, teachers with books, merchants with scales, smiths with hammers, carpenters with saws, and scribes with brushes and ink. I felt kind of funny when I saw those scribes, wondering if I'd join them there after my lady marries.

Day 150

We've all been in such a flurry only now am I able to write. Khan Tegus is back, wounded, a tenth of his warriors dead. They rode hard into Song for Evela, bringing in villagers and shutting the city gates behind them.

I spent an entire helpless day scrubbing so hard I feared I'd make holes in the pots, until at last Shria came for me. Since then I haven't spent much time here in my quiet little room. I only came now to get some sleep because I was so tired I was beginning to see frogs leaping about in the corner of my eye. It'd make me laugh if times weren't so scary.

Three days I've spent with the shaman healers in Khan Tegus's room, singing until my throat's fair scalded with songs. He bears an arrow wound through his side and it's turned to fever. His breath wheezes while he sleeps, a sound that makes my own skin hurt as if a thousand red ants bit me at once.

The shamans change his bandages, give him drinks, dance with their drums, pray toward the Sacred Mountain, burn incense, and read the cracks in fire-heated sheep bones for any signs of hope. I hold Tegus's warm hand and sing and sing. My lord, my poor lord. It's too much like my mama's end. Times there are these past days when I lay my head on his couch and begin to dream as soon as my eyes shut, and my dreams are always the blackness of the tower falling over all the world, an endless city of corpses, and my lord's body there, too, cast on the ground.

I need to try and rest so I can return to him and sing some more.

Day 151

The shaman healers dismissed me. Tegus isn't improving. My singing does nothing. So they said. And I was lying here on my horsehair blanket and believing them. But then I remembered how Tegus asked me to help Batu, how he said please. Please, Dashti. And I did. And he got better.

Then I got to wake-dreaming about a time when I was ten and I fell into a thorn bush and scraped my arm, and it swelled and swelled, my arm on fire, my whole body trembling with heat. Mama and I were alone on the edge of a great forest, with no one around to help for miles, but I remember how calm she was, how cool her hands on my face. And while I thrashed and sweated on my bed, she never stopped singing. On the third night, I woke from death dreams and looked up into her eyes, and I remember how I could see her confidence. She knew I could heal. So I curled up on her lap and felt her song move inside me until my skin cooled and I could sleep a healing sleep.

I'm going to go back to the khan's chamber now. I'm going to keep singing.

Day 153

It's still dark, the autumn morning too tired to rise, and I'm writing by firelight. The shaman healers feared that the khan's fever was the kind that comes with an open wound and stays and stays until it takes a warrior down days after battle. But at midnight his fever broke. They said it was a miracle, mumbled prayers to the north, then left or curled up to sleep on pallets on the floor.

I stayed by my lord's couch. It was the same couch where Batu had lain ill, where Tegus and I had leaned back together and stared at the fire, touching Batu's arm. This time, I touched the khan's arm and watched his chest rise and fall.

Over the past six days, I'd sung all the healing songs I knew, I'd stitched each one with my memories of sunlight, I'd poured any blue sky from my soul into the sounds. Now I was a snail's shell. There was nothing left for me to give.

So I sang him the nonsense song he'd given me in the tower. My voice was a horse's bray, I'm sure, raw with little sleep and so much singing. But I didn't want him to feel alone without any music to keep him company. "The piglet rolled while squealing, moving by snout and by jaw, happily snuffling for treats without use of hoof or paw." I sang it wrong. It needs a happy voice, the words jigging and the tune lilting up. All I could manage was a slow whisper, but I think it served.

I kept one hand on his arm and smoothed the hair back from his brow with the other. I sang. His eyes opened, and I should've withdrawn my hands. Really, I should've scuttled under the couch and hidden for shame. But I kept singing. And I kept one hand on his arm and the other on his forehead. And I stroked his hair back.

He watched me while I sang. He looked at my eyes. My heart felt so big, it hurt against my ribs. At last I felt some shame and started to pull away, but he put his hand over mine on his chest to hold me there longer. He knew I was just the mucker girl, the scrubber, and still he wanted to keep me close. I don't think I breathed for a long, long while.

I remembered in the tower before he came to visit, wondering if he'd been formed by Evela, goddess of sunlight. I think it might be true after all, because I began to squint wretchedly and couldn't look at his face.

When he slept again, I left him with the healers. I think I'll curl up in my horsehair blanket until the shivering in my limbs stops.

Day 155

This morning when I entered her khan's chamber, he was sitting up, his face not so pale. The icy fear that had lodged in my belly this last week at last began to melt. He was speaking with one of his chiefs, his face troubled, but when he saw me, he broke out in a grin so wide I have to believe it came right from his soul. Then he held his arms out before him, palms down, inviting me to clasp forearms as though we were of a clan, meeting again after a long absence.

"A warm greeting, Dashti," he spoke in the formal manner, though the cheerfulness in his smile made me think he wanted to laugh.

"A warm greeting, my lord," I replied, kneeling beside his bed and grasping his forearms with my palms up.

Then he did what I didn't expect from gentry to commoner—as we gripped arms, he pulled me closer, resting his cheek against mine, and inhaled through his nose, taking in the breath of my soul. I was too terrified to breathe. I hope he didn't notice that I didn't sniff as well, because refusing would mean insult, but I couldn't help but think, *Did he keep my shirt from the tower? Does he remember the scent?*

When he released me, he said, "So, just come from milking the sheep, have you?" which made me snort in laughter. It's a common mucker tease after a cheek greeting and means, of course, that I smell like a ewe, which I know I don't because I've been indoors for two weeks and bathed two days ago. His sly half smile made me think he'd actually sought out some other mucker and asked for something right silly to say to me.

So I answered, "I have, in fact. They send greeting to their brother Tegus."

Day 156

This morning, Tegus welcomed me again with an arm clasp and cheek touch. I wasn't startled this time, and I breathed in at his neck. How can I describe the scent of his skin? He smells something like cinnamon—brown and dry and sweet and warm. Ancestors, is it wrong for me to know that? To write it? Is it wrong for me to imagine laying my head on his chest and closing my eyes and breathing in his smell?

Yes, it is wrong. I won't think it again.

He told me he likes me close by, says my singing eases the pain. Even though I don't always sing. Mostly we talk. Often we laugh, at least until his arrow wound pierces him and the shaman healers shoo me away. But I always return before long, and they always let me back in. And I sing and we laugh.

I haven't touched him again, as I did when he

first woke from the fever sleep. I wonder if he remembers or if he thinks it was a dream.

Day 157

I've seen Lady Vachir at last, and she dresses in all
the splendor I would imagine for a lady of a realm.
Indigo powder colors her eyelids, sandlewood per-
fume wafts from her skin, and when she moves, the
dangling pearls in her hair click against her tortoise-
shell combs. One would imagine such finery could

make a lady happy. Not so. I find it easier to imagine a snake smiling than our Lady Vachir. Her mouth is stern, her eyes are sad, her hands lie in her lap like frozen things. For the past two days, she's been attending Tegus in his resting chamber. They brought in a second couch for her and her three lady's maids, and they sit with their backs straight, look at us, and whisper. Khan Tegus and I don't laugh much anymore.

When he's awake, I rest my hands on his belly wound and sing to his bones and skin, his muscles and blood. When he sleeps, I sit in the corner and do scribe work. To tell the truth, the scribbling has become about as much fun as picking lice out of a goat's hair. While I write, I can feel Lady Vachir's gaze prickling me. I don't like it much.

Today when the khan was asleep, Lady Vachir said, "My back pains me. What is that girl's name, the commoner there?"

Batu the war chief was present, and he answered, "Dashti, my lady."

"I want her to use her healing songs on me. Tell her to come to my chamber."

She and her ladies rose and left, and I supposed she meant me to follow, so I did. Halfway there, she claimed that her own chamber was being cleaned and I should take her to mine. So I led her to my little room and lay her on my horsehair blanket. Her three lady's maids stood around me like so many vultures waiting for something meaty to die. I placed my hands on the lady's back and sang the tune with the lilting high parts that says, "Tell me again, how does it go?"

When I finished, she stood and said, "I don't know why they let you hang about. Your song didn't make a drop of difference."

Well, that put some fire in my lungs, sure enough, so I said, "A song can only work if the hearer wills it. Do you perhaps enjoy the back pain? Or maybe your back didn't pain you to begin with?"

She slapped my mouth. What is it about gentry that they're always slapping people? It made me giggle, which made her glare. What's come over me to speak casually and laugh at an honored lady? As she swept out of the room, I noticed her gaze fall on this book, lying in the corner.

From now on, I'll keep it with me. Lady Vachir is the last person in the Eight Realms I'd want to see these words.

I like that woman about as much as I like skin rot in the summer. Maybe she rankles me so because she's standing between my lady and her beloved. Or maybe the woman is just plain unpleasant. I shouldn't be so hard, but there it is. I look at Lady Vachir and I see someone who loves nothing much, who's seen a great deal of death in a short amount of time, and rather than feel sorrow, has decided to turn into stone.

Day 159

These past days in my lord's chamber, all the talk is on Khasar. I try to ignore it and focus on what I'm copying on parchment, because there's nothing more frustrating than hearing of a problem you can't do anything to fix. But I can't help hearing some, and my mind keeps working over the trouble, like chewing on tough meat till my jaw's sore.

I don't like Khasar. I guess I've never been so terrified in my life as the time he flicked burning wood chips into our tower. His voice, even in memory, makes my bones shiver. The sounds of the healing songs remind the body of how it should be, but the sound of his voice had the opposite effect on me. Whatever he uttered, his laugh, his snarl, his words, seemed a song of ill. Just the memory of that sound greases my dreams some nights like fatty pot scrapings smeared on my hands.

The news today was that Khasar's warriors have rested and regrouped from their assault on Lady Vachir's land and are on the march again.

"He'd been laying siege on Beloved of Ris, my lord," said Batu, the war chief, who was healed and standing, strong as a yak after a good summer. "We thought he'd continue his siege through the winter, but he's moving again. Coming this way."

Khan Tegus winced as he sat upright. "I'd hoped to lead our army against him before the bitter cold comes, drive him away from Beloved of Ris. We can't risk the defeat of that realm and the warriors Khasar would add to his own."

"Is he marching to attack Song for Evela?" asked the chief of night, an old man whose fading brown eyes always seemed kindly to me. "Or is he returning to Thoughts of Under for winter?"

"There is no more Thoughts of Under," said Batu. "He's changed the name of his realm to Carthen's Glory."

That silenced everyone. Changed the name of his realm! I'd never heard of, never imagined such a thing. He must mean the change as a mighty prayer to Carthen, goddess of strength.

"Ancestors spare us," someone whispered.

They kept talking about strategy, numbers versus numbers, tactics if he marches on our khan's city and such, but my thoughts were running through a different forest. And though now I should be curled up in my horsehair blanket and long ago asleep, I had to write these thoughts first. They gnaw at me, like to chew me to bits before morning.

Khasar has betrayed Under, god of tricks, by abandoning his name, and pledged himself to Carthen. That makes me think the means to defeat him will be through trickery, not strength. He destroyed the realm of Titor, god of animals, and overthrew the land named for Goda, goddess of sleep. Animals, sleep, and trickery will not be his friends.

These thoughts feel true, but they also seem like the bones of some animal all in a jumble, and I can't see how they fit together and what they form. Maybe the Ancestors are trying to help me, if I could only see.

Day 161

Khasar's warriors are coming closer. It doesn't seem they mean to pass us by. I spend all my time in my lord's chamber now with his chiefs, Lady Vachir, and her whispering maids. When Tegus hurts too much to continue, I'm there to sing. But I miss the laughing parts.

Outside, the world is starting to crack with cold.

Day 162

Many were gathered in the khan's chamber today, the mood stiffer than winter laundry.

"His army is setting up camp outside our walls," said Batu. "They're well equipped with ghers and supplies. They can hunt our woods all winter and get on well."

"But we won't," said the town chief. She has gray and black hair, thick and tangled in braids all over her head. To me, her eyes look as dark as deep wells.

"We were prepared for a siege before," said the food chief, "but now with all the people we've taken in from Titor's Garden, Beloved of Ris, and Goda's Second Gift, not to mention our own villagers who have sought refuge inside the city walls, our stored food won't last two months."

"Longer if we eat the livestock," said the chief of animals. "But that choice is death still, just a slower death, if we have no animals next year."

"And there's the matter of the terror Khasar inspires," said the chief of light. He was resting his forehead on his templed fingers and just then didn't look much as if he were filled with sunshine. "Your warriors brought back tales of Khasar in battle, his ferocity, his eerie strength. And other rumors fill the barracks—the midnight killings in Beloved of Ris, how sentries and warriors disappeared from their posts and their bodies were found with their throats and organs eaten away. These stories will spread throughout the city and cause panic when Khasar attacks. Panic can defeat us as surely as lack of food."

"Worse news," said Batu. "The strange killings have already begun here. This morning, two men were found outside the city gates, ravaged as if by a wild beast."

Did Khasar have some dark alliance with predatory animals? How could he make a wild wolf attack on his command? My thoughts took me back to the tower, and I was hearing in memory the screams that night when a wolf howled. The screams of our guards who never appeared again. It was not a comfortable memory and it made me want to curl up somewhere with a wall at my back.

The chiefs had gone quiet and Khan Tegus was staring at the fire. At length he said, "Batu, what do you recommend?"

"We must attack. Now, before full winter. There's no choice."

"Holy one?" Tegus spoke to a shaman crouched before the fire.

The shaman was removing sheep anklebones from the embers and spreading them out on the floor. He hopped around, squinting at the cracks in the bones, humming sometimes and moaning others. We all waited.

"Foretelling is never exact, my khan," said the shaman. He peered up through his hat tassels. "But your victory won't come from strength, so I see in the bones."

"But it's not exact," said the town chief, "and if we have no other way—"

"Strength can't be your friend," said the shaman, "not since Khasar pledged himself to the goddess Carthen."

"That's right!" I said. I did shout out those words just like that, with all those people present. The shaman spoke the thoughts I'd been thinking, and now in my mind the jumble of bones was beginning to click together. "He'll have Carthen on his side, but he betrayed Under, god of tricks. My lord, I think that might be the way to defeat him."

Some scowled at my outburst, but Tegus asked me, "What hope do you see, Dashti?"

"With no offense to the holy one or to Dashti,"

said Batu, "this isn't the time to bet our lives, our entire realm, on uncertain foretelling or mucker faith. We can't hesitate with this monster, my lord. His assault is terrible. His warriors attack night and day. All say it's as though he never sleeps. We must hit Khasar from the front with every warrior we have."

The khan nodded. "First, Dashti, tell me your thoughts."

I smiled at him. I couldn't help it. He makes me smile. "In battle, we'd have no chance. As the holy one said, with Carthen as his ally, no one can defeat him by means of arms. But Under is bound to be angered by the betrayal. With Under's blessing, I think you can trick Khasar."

"How do you propose we trick him?"

I didn't know, to be honest. I still don't. I just felt coolness and motion inside, like underground rivers running through me, and a sureness that it could be done. Something to do with Under, some trickery involving animals. Perhaps the very wolf Lord Khasar uses to kill warriors at night would turn on him. And somehow, we could make that happen. And then I remembered what Saren once said about Khasar, how he ripped out the throat of a goat. I'd thought she was just tower-addled at the time, but I begin to wonder what she may know.

"Well?" said the town chief. "We're waiting for your cunning plan."

I looked at the shaman for help, but he shrugged. Apparently the sheep bones didn't tell him anything more.

I cleared my throat. "Let me think about it. I—"

One of the chiefs laughed. The chief of animals, I think it was. The chief of camel dung and jackasses. I'm sitting in my room under the horsehair blanket, and I feel that laugh still crawling all over me.

Later

After last I wrote, I begged Cook for a moment with Saren. I took her into the sugar closet, where I feel suffocated but she seems to calm. Cook used to keep it locked, the sugar safe from prying fingers, but this one's empty now, what with traders from the south avoiding the Eight Realms since Khasar began his warring. I took Saren's hands. I met her eyes. She's more relaxed of late, but she set to blinking when she heard me mention Khasar's name.

"My lady, once you told me that Khasar is a beast, that you saw him tear a goat's throat with his teeth. I need to know what you meant. Please tell me."

Her eyes went so wide I thought she'd never blink again, and she shook her head.

"He's here, my lady. His armies are camped outside the wall. They'll do here what they did to Titor's Garden if we don't—"

That was stupidity on my part. I should've kept that news silent, because then she set to shaking and moaning. "He's here, he's coming in for me, I knew he would, he won't let me be, I'd rather be dead—"

"Please, my lady, help me stop him. You know something about Khasar that no one else knows, don't you? What is it?"

"I can't remember," she said.

I was cruel then. I should've spared her the memory, but I pressed. I reminded her of how I've cared for her, how I stayed with her when all others left. I took her shoulders and held her, and I demanded, I ordered her as she would order me.

"By the Ancestors, Saren, tell me!"

"I'm trying, Dashti! I am. I'm trying. I try to think but my thoughts slip out of my hands and everything's darkness and . . ."

She started to cry, which made me realize I hadn't seen her cry in weeks. My poor lady, who is just chaff in the breeze. I held her as I used to do when she was tower-addled; I rocked her and sang the calming song, "Oh, moth on a wind, oh, leaf on a stream." Patience, I told myself, though the knowledge of Khasar's nearness pressed on me, like being out in the heaviest of cold.

I placed my hand on her forehead, and I wove the calming song into the tune for Goda's prayer. The goddess of sleep knows the mind.

After a time, Saren shuddered but stopped crying. Her eyes closed, and she leaned against me as if too tired to sit. While I was singing, My Lord the cat nosed the door ajar and leaped onto her lap, purring under her hand.

She took a deep breath, leaned into me more fully, and told the story she'd been keeping for seven years. "I was twelve years old and was visiting Lord Khasar with my father. His house was vast and cold, like my father's but darker, heavier. We ate a huge feast. I knew my father had hopes of betrothing me to Khasar, but I didn't pay any mind. It seemed as though it had nothing really to do with me. They talked and I ate and played with a little dog that begged under the table. Sometimes I felt Khasar watching me.

"I had a room to myself while we stayed in his house. I thought it was such fun at first. I'd never been alone before, and I could run around the room and climb on the furniture and not worry about my maids and my father and what they thought of me. But at sundown, one of Khasar's men came to my door. His name was Chinua. He was Khasar's war chief and had constantly been at his side. He said my father and Khasar sent him to fetch me."

Her forehead furrowed, but she didn't open her eyes. "I was afraid," she stated simply. "I thought my father would have me do something humiliating before Khasar, like make me dance while they laughed. Or he might slap me, just for show. He never slapped me when we were alone, only in front of people. While I didn't dare refuse my father's call, I did wonder why Chinua seemed full of some secret joke.

"He took me to a courtyard outside Lord Khasar's house, hidden from the eyes of windows. My father wasn't there. Lord Khasar was. He called me Saren. He said, 'Fitting that a girl named for moonlight should see me as only the moon knows me. What do you say, Chinua, is it time to show myself to this moon?' He smiled as the sun finished setting, then he took off all his clothes until he was naked."

"Naked?" This part surprised me. To be naked outside is utter submission, and to be unclothed before anyone besides family is humiliation. "That doesn't sound like Khasar. Why would he willingly debase himself?"

Saren shook her head. "It was different with him. It was as though he was naked to embarrass *me*. It was so strange how Khasar just stood there and laughed at my discomfort. So strange, and I was too afraid to do anything, even to look away. Then the last of the sunlight faded, and I realized why he'd taken off his clothes. It was so they wouldn't rip." She shook. "In the darkness he changed, Dashti. Right in front of me, Khasar changed from a man into a beast. A wolf."

She was quiet for a time and I was glad she was. I had to make sense of this in my own head. In one way it seemed impossible, and in another I felt as if I'd known this all along.

"At first I thought he meant to kill me," Saren continued. "But then I noticed a goat on a tether, and so did Khasar the wolf. Chinua held my head and made me watch while the wolf devoured the animal. I was sure I'd be next, but after the goat was a wrecked carcass, Chinua moved us behind a fire. The wolf ignored us, sniffed the air, and ran off into the woods.

"Chinua laughed and laughed, and while he laughed he told me things. That his lord had gone off to hunt in the woods until sunup. That his lord had made quite a bargain with the desert shamans and now was the greatest hunter in all the realms. He said, weren't we lucky to be the only ones alive to know Lord Khasar's secret? Once his lord had allowed another girl to witness his transformation, but she'd told a boy. Afterward, both were found in a pile of their own innards, and if I ever told a soul, I'd be the next goat."

Saren's eyes fluttered, then she closed them again. "I saw Lord Khasar the next morning, and he smiled at me and touched my braids and told me I was beautiful. He'd eaten that goat and hunted other things in the woods as well, and yet when I looked in his eyes, I knew he's never full."

"He killed our tower guards," I said, realizing it as I spoke. "As a wolf, he attacked them, and all those guards with their weapons couldn't kill him. You knew all along and yet you didn't dare tell me."

She sat up and opened her eyes, speaking straight at me with no fear. "I'm telling you now. Khasar becomes a beast at night. In the dark, he's a wolf. I want you to know. I guess he'll kill me like the goat now that I've told, but I don't care anymore. Even if I have to die, I want it to be over. I'm tired of being afraid."

"I'll find a way to end it," I told her.

She rested her head on my shoulder again and didn't cry. I thanked her and I sang to her, and she sighed like a traveler who can rest at last. My poor lady. All she's been for years is a frightened little girl. I've promised her I'll make it better, and I will. I must.

So, how does one trick a wolf?

Day 163

I'm alone in a room, though not the small clean room, not the kitchen, and not my lord's resting chamber. There are windows, but these look out on the city, these are high up. It's not a tower, not quite, though it seems as much like a prison. Just now, I understand my lady's plea that she wanted to die. My stomach feels like the winter sky.

After Saren remembered Khasar's horror, I passed the night drowsing between ideas, then waking again with thoughts of what to do. What to do? Could I trick him into becoming a wolf by daylight? Is there a way to sing him into that shape? What would happen if he did become a wolf under the sun? And how could I get close enough to make it happen?

As soon as it was light enough, I went to Khan Tegus's chamber to share what I knew, but it was filled with chiefs and shamans, and of course Lady Vachir and her vulture maids sitting on their perch.

As I entered, the war chief was saying, "He's

declaring he won't attack Song for Evela if we give him Lady Saren."

I stood in the threshold, though I know it's bad luck. I couldn't move, not forward or back. My mama said I'm as brave as the lead gazelle with hunters on her tail, but I wasn't then. Since coming to Song for Evela, too many times I've put my mama to shame.

"Lady Saren?" The khan rubbed his forehead. "Is Khasar truly insane? He has Lady Saren already, if he hasn't killed her yet."

"What do you mean Khasar has Lady Saren?" I asked. I just couldn't keep quiet.

Some of the chiefs glared at me for interrupting, but her khan answered.

"Dashti, I didn't see you. Have you heard of the lady in the tower? I knew her." He glanced at Lady Vachir before continuing. "I visited her one autumn. When I returned to Titor's Garden in the spring, Khasar was at the tower before me, and two hundred of his men camped with him. I'd only thirty men and couldn't risk attacking."

He came back! I smiled at him. I wanted him to know how wonderful he was, but he was looking out the window.

"Surely Khasar was there to break her out," he said, "take her back to his own realm."

"But now he's asking for her," said the town chief.

"Maybe he didn't take her." Tegus drummed the pane with his fingers. "But if he didn't, where is she?"

There was silence for a few moments, and my soul rumbled inside of me, rolling around like a ball in a box, shaking my bones.

I'd sworn to protect my lady. I'd said I'd claim her name and title and see if the khan would welcome her. I knew I should speak up now, the Ancestors designed this very moment to allow me to do my duty. But instead, I quaked and stared at my feet. And the moment passed.

"He claims he has one hundred villagers on neck ropes," said Batu, "ones too slow to flee before his army's advance. He's shouting that he'll catapult them into our city if we don't turn over the lady. Scouts confirm the hostages."

"Ancestors," sighed an old chief, rubbing his back as if the news made him ache.

The khan stared hard at Batu and finally asked, "And what's the part that you aren't telling me?"

Batu sighed. "He said he wanted Lady Saren, but he'd accept you, my lord. He goaded, said a true khan would give his own life to protect his people."

"A true khan . . . ," said Tegus.

Silence. The fire in the hearth shivered.

"I don't advise believing anything Khasar says, my lord," said Batu. "He still believes if he kills you and conquers Song for Evela, he can take the title of khan, and after that I doubt he'd stop until he seizes all the Eight Realms and declares himself Great Khan. Even if we had Lady Saren to release to him, I can't believe he'd give up his war."

"But those hundred villagers . . ." Tegus covered his face with a hand, shaking his head. "And where is she? Where's Saren all this time?"

"Here." I couldn't believe I'd spoken it even as I did, and my stomach ached and my blood stopped running in my veins. "Here," I said again, just to make sure I really had. I swore an oath to my lady, and I have to believe that if I do the right thing, the Ancestors will take care of the rest.

Everyone was staring at me. At least, I felt like they were, but I was only watching Tegus. I'd grown used to his amused expression when he looked at me. Now the confusion on his face felt as unpleasant as a slap.

"Dashti?" he said. "What are—"

"I'm Lady Saren." I was amazed how sure I sounded as I spoke. "Dashti is my maid's name."

He took a step forward, stopped. Everyone still stared. I was waiting for laughter, or maybe to be tied up with their sashes like the assassin who'd stabbed Batu. Tegus took another step forward. I would've accused him of dancing if I hadn't been shaking with the fear that he'd frown at me and demand I be strung up on the south wall.

"Khasar didn't take us from the tower," I explained. "He just came to mock us. We wouldn't go with him willingly, so he left us to rot. When we ran out of food, we broke our way out. Titor's Garden was razed, so we came here, but I wasn't sure if . . . you were engaged to Lady Vachir, and I didn't know if . . ."

My throat burned with the lies. Tegus still just stared.

Lady Vachir stood up from her couch with a not very nice expression. I guess she wasn't feeling much fondness for me. I guess she was imagining me on a spit, slowly turning over a fire. Truth be told, that's pretty much how I felt.

"You broke out?" asked Tegus. He took another step closer.

Why wasn't he calling me a liar? I look nothing like Lady Saren, and surely at a glance anyone can see I'm not gentry.

"It was the rats, my lord," I said. "They ate our food, but they also dug a way through the bricks. Funny how the thing I thought would kill us actually saved us in the end, isn't it? The cat you gave me was a brilliant rat hunter! But he was chased off when Khasar came back, and in his absence the rats took over. I was sorry to leave the pine bough behind in the tower. I kept it those three years."

"The pine bough." He stepped even closer. He took my hands, lifted them to his face, and breathed in through his nose, the formal greeting between gentry. Despite it all, a thrill tickled me.

"Lady Saren? After all these years to see you for the first time with Lord Khasar at the city walls. . . ."

"My lord?"

"Hearing your voice in the tower, I'd imagined meeting you so many times. And now you're Dashti . . . I . . . my lady." He shook his head and winced and smiled all at once. "I'm not sure if I'm standing on my feet or on my head."

So. That jumble of animal bones was beginning to come together. He'd never seen Lady Saren before. He'd never seen her! They'd never met when they began to communicate through letters. The only time he'd spoken with Lady Saren was in the tower. But it had been me. Ancestors, what a thought.

"I should've come forward before," I said, "but I was afraid. I'm sorry, my lord. Please forgive—"

"Don't you dare ask my forgiveness! After abandoning you, leaving you to Khasar and rats and darkness and starvation, all because I was too afraid. I'm unforgivable, Dashti . . . my lady. But will *you*?" He knelt at my feet, he held my hands against his face as he bowed before me. His voice broke. "Can you forgive me?"

Everyone began talking at once, which was just as well, since my breath had frozen solid inside me and I couldn't make a sound above a croak. Lady Vachir wanted to know who I was to threaten her betrothal, and Batu proposed that all questions of betrothal be set aside until Khasar was vanquished, and all the chiefs who didn't know the story of Lady Saren were clamoring for explanations, so others began to explain.

And all the while, Tegus held my hands to his face. I didn't mean to stroke his cheek—my thumb moved of its own accord, I swear. He smiled up at me, and my face felt hot.

I tugged him to his feet, saying, "Please, my lord, please don't kneel to me."

He arose and clasped my hands inside his. We were standing so close.

238

"I'm sorry," he whispered beneath the clamor around us. "My lady, I am so sorry." Then he grinned. "But even more, I'm happy. You're Lady Saren. And you're alive and well and here. Thank the Ancestors, you're here."

I felt ready to fall apart with all the elation and frustration and fear. The lie was heaps of cold mud on top of me, fit to suffocate me dead. Shria began talking about getting me into garments befitting my position and letting me rest in a proper chamber and chiefs were begging they return to the matter of war when I remembered my purpose.

"He's a wolf." I spoke quickly before they could interrupt, my voice tumbling over the noise. "Khasar never sleeps, he fights by day and hunts by night. He's a skinwalker, empowered by a desert shaman ritual to add the strength of a wolf to his own. That's why he's so fierce in battle. And at night, he takes wolf form, killing by stealth and spreading fear. But this might be the means to trick him. Send me down to him, send him Lady Saren, and let me—"

It was as much as I could explain before Tegus refused to let me anywhere near that butcher and Lady Vachir objected to my presence and the chiefs were in an uproar about the battle plan, that they must attack Khasar, that his deadline was for tomorrow noon and the warriors were preparing and needed the khan's attention now.

Sometimes I think they're all ridiculous. There I was, a sensible person with thoughts in my head, offering a solution. And they wouldn't listen. What aggravation, to believe I can help and yet not be allowed.

Shria took me by the shoulders and rushed me away, saying, "We'd no idea, my lady, if we'd known, my lady . . ." As I left, I caught sight of Batu, who seemed to be considering me seriously.

And here I am, in a different room, this one with a low couch and a silk coverlet, a lacquered table and a porcelain bowl filled with nuts for cracking. It's higher up in the khan's house, its window larger. At my request, Shria brought me my things—the horsehair blanket, my wool cloak and my boots, and my ink and brushes.

"Here's Sar, my lady, who I realize now must be your maid," and Shria ushered Saren into the room, still wearing her apron and smelling of kitchen smoke.

It was rather awkward while Shria remained with Saren pretending to be a lady's maid but mostly standing there staring at me like some baby animal. When the white-haired woman finally left, Saren collapsed on my pallet.

"I did it, my lady," I said.

She stared at the ceiling. "Thank you."

We were quiet.

"Would you like some nuts?"

"No," she said. Then, "Cook was having me decorate a serving platter for dinner. I'd like to go back to it. And make sure My Lord the cat gets his meat shavings."

"Of course."

So she left. And I'm relieved because I have enough thoughts and fear quakings to make me happy to be alone. It's night now, and even from here I can detect the bleary lights beyond the city walls. Khasar's men and their fires, their numbers rivaling the stars, laughing back at the eternal blackness of the night sky.

I'm afraid to put down my brush and ink. I'm afraid I'll be chilled by the quiet that comes after my brush ceases stroking parchment, that the silence will lower me into the night like into a grave. Now I'm being dramatic, I guess. I should say that I'm just plain afraid. I've got to do something and I don't know if I can.

Day 164

Or is it still yesterday? I write by firelight. I write because I want these ink strokes to give me courage,

241

as I seem to be lacking it. My veins feel dry and dusty of blood. Not much of a mucker, am I, to be so terrified? I've tried laughing at myself, but it hasn't helped yet.

An hour ago, I went in search of Batu, the war chief. I woke Shria, and she told me where to find his room. She thinks me gentry, she'll do what I ask. What an unhappy laugh that gives me.

Batu didn't seem surprised to see me at his door in the middle of the night. He stepped into the hall so neither of us would invoke the bad luck of the threshold.

"Did you promise the khan anything regarding me?" I asked before revealing my plan.

"No, I didn't."

"Then I'll tell you that I'm going down to Lord Khasar. I've been praying to Under all night. He hasn't answered me, but when does the god of tricks offer signs to his petitioners?"

"Indeed."

I cleared my throat. My voice was sounding an awful lot like a rat's squeak, and I've had enough of that noise for a lifetime. "I'm going of my own will, as Lady Saren. Would it be against your oath to Khan Tegus to help me?"

Batu frowned at me a good long while. Then he

shook his head. "No, it would not. But what do you plan to do?"

"Get close enough to Khasar to sing. A song can't force Khasar to do anything, but if I sing to the wolf inside him, maybe the wolf will choose to come out."

"And then what will happen?"

"Something," I said with much conviction to hide the feeble answer. "None of his men know he's a skinwalker, except his war chief. At least, that was true a few years ago, and I think it must still be so. And if they find out—"

"Who knows," said Batu, "it might cause them to revere Khasar all the more."

"Would your warriors follow you if they believed you'd traded the life of your soul to desert shamans?"

Batu considered. "Their loyalty would be dented, no question, and after a time I believe they would abandon me. But in the midst of a war, they might follow me into battle all the same."

"Yes, but . . ." I didn't know how to form my impressions into words. "But if they actually saw him. I mean, how would you react if you saw someone change into a wolf? He's never a wolf by day, so he'd be confused and they'd be confused and . . . and . . ."

What would happen then? Would he attack his own men? Would they fight back? I don't know. But

I have these ideas, and I have a strong body to carry them out, and a reason to do it. How can I not?

"My lady, I don't think you should throw away your life, and I don't think I should take your hand and lead you to your end."

He put a hand on my shoulder as if to usher me back to my room, but I grabbed the doorpost.

"Did you see Khan Tegus today, when you told him Khasar would take his life instead of Saren's? Is there any chance that Tegus will offer himself to save those hundred villagers? For the war, for this realm, isn't Tegus more important than any risk I might take?"

Batu shut his eyes. He was tired, I could see that now. We all are lately, I guess. At least he didn't argue with me again.

We agreed to meet at the kitchen door at dawn. He'll lead me to the east city gate and tell the guards to let me pass. From there, I'll go alone. I'll walk toward Khasar's camp from the east, so the sun will rise behind me, granting me a shadow on my face. I'll wear my hair down and loose, so he won't see me well enough to know the lie. Unlike Tegus, Khasar has seen Saren. I'll go barefoot so he'll see my naked ankles beneath my cloak and know I am a girl and not a warrior, and so perhaps let me get close enough to sing. I'll go alone.

Carthen, goddess of strength, I need your smile more than Khasar does. Evela, give me a bright sun and a dark shadow, and grant me a powerful song. Under, I plead the honor of being the dagger of your revenge.

Later

Is it still the same day? It feels years later. I can't sleep tonight in this strange place, in yet another new room. I managed to keep my book, and I have a new brush and ink and nothing to do but fret and write, so I'll tell you all that's happened. Ancestors have mercy.

When I met Batu at the kitchen door, I brought Mucker with me. His exhales were billows of white, and he leaned his head against me like an enormous cat. Titor, but I love that beast.

"I'll ride the yak to the gate," I said.

I didn't say that I hoped riding a yak, Titor's favorite animal, might grant me a kind glance from him, because Batu didn't seem to believe in "mucker faith."

And I didn't say that I wanted to put my fingers on an animal's neck to feel some steady comfort or I was likely to break down and sob like a newborn. I certainly didn't say that.

Batu led the yak through the streets. The ways were narrow, clogged with the ghers of refugees, and by the time we reached the east city gate, the sun had cleared the horizon. I couldn't feel its heat. The air was ice that seemed ready to break under my fist. My hands were shaking like to come off my arms, though I don't think I can blame the shaking on just the cold.

Batu spoke to the gate guards, and they inched the gates open. Two arrow shots away, Khasar's warriors camped. They resembled ants in an anthill, for all that I could ever hope to count their number.

Batu put his hand on Mucker's neck. "Are you certain, my lady? There's little chance Khasar will keep his word once he has you."

"I'm wagering on the god of tricks today," I said.

"That's a poor wager," one of the gate guards muttered.

I slipped off my boots then slid off Mucker's back, and the moment my bare feet touched earth, they went numb with cold. I patted Mucker's nose once before beginning the walk across the empty field toward Khasar.

How can I say what it was like? Cold. Long. Lonely as ghosts. I guess it was about the worst moment of my life, almost as hard as singing my mama into the next Realm—and much colder. Khasar and his men were so far off it felt like forever to get there, and even though I wasn't eager to arrive, the journey itself was misery. Does fright hurt? It did then, it did for me, in my stomach and in my limbs. And it didn't help that my feet were so frozen I couldn't sense where they ended and the ground began, twice causing me to trip. I'd really rather not have fallen on my face in front of thousands of warriors who were waiting to kill me. Under seemed to be playing tricks on me, and I began to doubt that I'd any hope. But by then I was already there.

"Lord Khasar!" I shouted. At least that part of my plan worked. I'd intended to shout his name and it actually came right out.

"Khan Khasar, you meant to say." He stepped out of his gher but stayed so far back, I couldn't make out his face. I knew his voice, of course. It was turning my bones to soup. "I'm letting you live for the moment because I'm curious about this girl who crosses my battlefield. Just what are you offering? I won't pay."

His men laughed roughly. Khasar lifted his sword, making some call I didn't understand, and two dozen of his men moved into a half circle between me and Khasar, fully armored, bows pulled back, swords bare.

"Take another step and I'll show the Eternal Blue Sky the color of your liver. If Tegus thinks to use an assassin, he'll not fool me by sending a woman with a poisoned dagger."

I stopped walking, gripping my cloak tighter. The cold was slithering up my bare legs.

"Chinua, check her," said Khasar.

"Show me your hands," said a man to Khasar's right, a tall, thin man. I figured this was Khasar's war chief, the one who'd taken Saren to watch Khasar become a wolf.

I raised my hands and for some wild reason, I

found myself remembering how Tegus had once called them beautiful. Spared from the scrubbing waters of late, they've softened, though if Khasar looked too closely, he'd see the scars and calluses.

"Now deliver your message before I gut —"

"My lord, it's me, Lady Saren." My voice went soft. I was ashamed to tell a lie right beneath the Eternal Blue Sky. Lies are for dark holes and rooms without candles.

"Speak up!"

"I'm Lady Saren," I said, louder.

"Lady Saren." He snarled a laugh. "I knew that khan wouldn't be able to resist breaking you out. Take off your hood, I want to see your scared cow eyes."

I pulled my hood back. My hair hung down, the sun was behind me, and I hoped he was still too far back to see. I thought I should say something quickly to prove I was Lady Saren, something true, before he could see in my face who I was not.

"The day you threw flames into the tower," I said, "the day you tried to smoke me like winter meat, I guess I've never been so scared in my life."

He laughed. I hate his laugh.

"All you are is fear," he said.

"I believe that was also the day you bathed in my waste," I couldn't help adding.

249

I was happy to see him flinch. I guess he didn't much like my mentioning that in front of his men.

"You told me you'd only take me if I came willingly," I said. "And here I am."

I started toward him, but three of his men moved to block my way.

Though he thought me the frail Lady Saren, he still wouldn't let me near. He was too clever to risk the chance I might have a hidden weapon. This morning before going out, that possibility had haunted me, so I'd disrobed completely under my cloak. I'd been praying since that I wouldn't have to take it off, but that ultimate submission seemed to be the only way he'd think me harmless, the only way to get near enough to sing.

I shut my eyes as I unhooked the neck clasp and let the warmth fall to the ground. Winter blasted my skin, and the cold shot up from my feet through my entire body.

Khasar stared, suddenly with nothing to say.

"You see I'm hiding no weapons, my lord." I tried to sound brave as gentry, but I was shivering so hard, my voice warbled like a bird's, my words knocking against each other. I had to bite my tongue to bleeding to keep from picking my cloak back up, wrapping it around myself, curling up to hide. "You see I submit to you. I'm here of my own will, as you wanted. I'm sacrificing myself for this realm. If you are a man of honor, before the Ancestors, under the Eternal Blue Sky, you'll keep your word. Take me and leave this realm in peace."

He didn't say anything. He stared at me. His men looked away, at the ground, at the clouds. Though hard warriors, I think they couldn't help being embarrassed for the poor naked girl. There was some revenge in this, I realized, remembering how Lord Khasar had stood naked before my lady. But I couldn't glory in it. The shame hurt me like the cold, and I trembled inside and out and winced when tears burned my eyes.

"Please don't make me stand here like this," I said, my words shaking. I didn't mean to beg, but there it came. "Please say you accept my sacrifice and let me put my cloak back on. Please."

He started walking toward me now. Slowly. His men stepped aside.

"You surprise me, Lady Saren."

He kept coming nearer.

"I never expected you to do anything but tremble and cry. Though I see you're trembling, where are the tears? Ah, I think I see one. That's better."

And nearer. My stomach quivered, my blood was hot. This was the moment. I bowed my head, as if meekly. The sunlight was strong behind me, Evela was smiling on my hope, but I knew the moment he saw my face, he'd kill me. He was near enough now that through my hair I could make out his own features. I can't say if he was handsome or ugly. He looked like pain to me. Then I noticed one detail—he had three thin white scars down his cheek, like the marks a cat might leave. It seems My Lord had drawn some blood that night he escaped the wolf's jaws. The thought gave me a gust of warm courage.

Before Khasar's hands reached me, I had to act.

"Witness all!" I lifted my arms and knelt, the frosty grass snapped like glass under my knees. "See Lady Saren surrender to Khan Khasar. I sing the song of submission."

Here was the trick. I don't know a song of submission. Instead, I began to sing the song of the wolf.

"Yellow eyes, blink the night," I sang. "Two paws in, two paws gone," while praying that there were no muckers among his warriors, that they wouldn't know what it was I sang. I remembered the voices of my brothers chanting those words, yelling them at the night to save the sheep, felt that childhood tune hum inside me now as if in harmony. I reached forward, I touched Khasar's boots, hoping the contact would make the song stronger.

Khasar stared down at me and did nothing, his face puzzled, his body rigid. I think I understood him then—I think he felt that something was wrong but he couldn't allow himself to be afraid, not of me, not of a naked girl singing. And because he did nothing to stop me, neither did his men. I kept singing, calling the wolf out of the man.

Too late Khasar asked, "What are you—"

He didn't finish his question, because his head was thrown back, and he stared up, in pain or thrill I don't know. I almost stopped singing then, my limbs shook so that the ache was nearly unbearable. I didn't know what would happen. Would the wolf in Khasar hear my song and flee its daylight form? Would it come out under the sun?

With my voice I sang, and with my heart I prayed. Titor, god of animals, whose realm this man destroyed. Under, god of tricks, whose name this man cast off. Goda, goddess of sleep, I gave you a sleepless night in prayer. Evela, my lady, goddess of sunlight and songs, give me voice. Ancestors, let me sing this man into his animal form, his sleepless form of night, trick him into it under this sunlight.

I sang to him the song of the wolf.

He stumbled back a step, but it was the most he

could manage. All his force seemed focused on trying to hold his shape. His men were still looking away, ashamed of my shame, unaware of their lord's danger. Then Khasar groaned.

"My lord? Khan Khasar?" Chinua asked, as if beginning to wonder if something was wrong. The rest didn't suspect me still, I think. I'd completely debased myself, I'd become a thing too low to contemplate. Still, I guessed I wouldn't have long. The moment they thought me dangerous, they'd let their arrows fly.

Louder I sang. I stood, trembling for cold and fear, and I put my hands on his chest. So close I was, he could've snapped my neck by accident. If he'd looked, he'd have seen the lie in my face. But his neck arched and his glance flung up toward the sky. My voice quavered so that on the low notes it was nothing but a rasp, two stones grating together.

Please, I prayed. *Please change. Hurry. Become that wolf. Now, now.*

"My lord? Are you all right?" asked Chinua. He stepped forward two paces and pulled his bow back tighter. "I think you'd better stand back now, girl."

But I couldn't stand back until Khasar was gone where he couldn't hurt Tegus or make my lady quake or sneak into my nightmares. I clung to Khasar, so the warriors couldn't shoot at me without risking their lord.

"The night, the night!" I sang, and my voice was getting more desperate. I knew I didn't sound very meek anymore, but the wolf in Khasar wasn't coming out. "The night drips from your teeth. The night melts from your eyes. Yellow eyes!"

"Stand back," said Chinua, "or your eyes will be strung together on my arrow!"

He aimed at my head, I screamed my song, and Khasar thrust back his head and howled. Not at the moon, not at the shifting stars, but howled right at the Eternal Blue Sky.

That, I thought *should get the Ancestors' attention.*

Khasar pulled out of my grip, and I dropped flat to the ground just as an arrow whisked over me. I kept singing. And Khasar kept thrashing. His men were advancing, but for the moment they forgot me in favor of their lord, who had begun to screech and howl, his hands clawing the air. I held no weapon; they must not have understood that I could harm him. So I sang on, though I don't know how I found any voice with all the shaking and barely a breath trickling into my lungs.

Then the change happened. It really did. I'd believed Saren when she'd told me what she'd seen, or I'd thought I had, but until I saw the change myself,

I guess I hadn't truly understood. Just the sight of its wrongness made my stomach seize up, and I would've lost my breakfast if I'd had any.

I don't think I can describe the sound of flesh bulging and ripping, or the smell that clouded around Khasar, strange and rancid. I can say that his face thrust out, his back hunched with fur, his clothing tore, his armor bent and groaned before popping off. He dropped down on all fours and where Khasar had stood, a wolf now growled.

Khasar the wolf was enormous, as tall as an antelope, as fat as a mare, with jaws that could take down the largest yak. The size, the sheer menace of the thing made me quake, and the song choked in my throat. His men hollered and jumped back from the snarls, the teeth, the daggered paws.

"It's our lord!" shouted Chinua. "Do not harm him!"

Here's where my plan took the greatest risk. What would the wolf do? I was bargaining that the wolf who had snarled at me in the tower was more instinct than thought, that he loses his humanness when he's a wolf. Saren's story suggested such, when Chinua moved them behind a fire to protect them from his lord. Here was my hope—that Khasar the wolf would now attack his own men.

"It is our lord," Chinua was shouting. "Do not harm him!"

Chinua ran about, bellowing, trying to get warriors to move so the wolf would have an escape, but the camp completely ringed the woods. With city wall before us and forty thousand warriors and their ghers and animals all around, there was nowhere for the beast to flee. He paced and growled and wiped his face against his legs as if the sunlight were painful.

My plan was failing. The warriors kept their swords and arrows pointed at the wolf but didn't strike, and the wolf just snarled and snapped at nothing.

"Change back, Lord Khasar," Chinua said. "It's day! Change, my lord, change."

He's going to turn back, I thought. And then he'll kill me or worse.

His men now knew that he was a wolf skin-walker, but the warriors weren't fleeing their posts. As Batu said, there was the possibility that they'd revere him even more. I'd lost, I'd lost.

The failure was painful and I was so cold, I moved to crawl back into my cloak. That was a stupid thing to do. Stupid. Because then the wolf noticed me.

His eyes were on me, and he crouched and snarled.

Sing, Dashti, I told myself. *Push him back with your song. Sing!*

But I was so cold, so terrified, my voice iced in my throat. I couldn't squeak even a word. So I tried to run. I didn't make it three steps.

He pounced, landing on my leg, and I heard a crunch before I felt pain. His foul breath filled my mouth as he snapped in my face, and my stomach tried to vomit. I turned my head as he lunged. The sides of our skulls collided. I could taste blood.

Then, the eerie whistle of an arrow scratched the air. The arrow nipped the beast in the rear and he yelped and turned. His warriors stared back, shaking. One warrior held a bow with no arrow. Maybe it had been a mistake and the bowstring had slipped in his fingers. Maybe he had a sister or daughter my age and thought of her when the wolf leaped on me. Or maybe it had been Under's doing. However it was, Ancestors, please bless that man.

The wolf made a new noise in his throat now, one of hunger and rage. He turned his jaws toward the warriors, and he lunged.

"Don't shoot him," Chinua yelled, but three men, their eyes wide with terror, began emptying their quivers. It didn't matter—the wolf leaped and rolled at incredible speed, and nothing could touch him. When one arrow grazed his leg, the wolf wailed in rage. He sprang, his jaws tearing out the throats of two men.

More arrows cut the air, and the wolf's attack became so swift and deadly, several warriors lay bleeding before I could even comprehend what was happening.

The wolf was smearing his muzzle in the blood of another soldier when at last one of the arrows struck him hard, then another and another. He roared and clawed at the warriors, killing two more. The men were running back, letting arrows fly as they tried to get out of his reach. Chinua was yelling something, but so was everyone else. Another arrow struck the wolf, another, and another. He howled and snarled, running a circle in mad fury.

He was too wounded to make chase, and all the warriors had retreated beyond his reach. That's when his horrible eyes found me again. I'd managed to pull my cloak on and was trying to drag myself away, but I couldn't stand, I couldn't run. How I prayed to Carthen, goddess of strength! I wept so hard my throat ached, though I was too cold to make tears.

The wolf padded toward me, stuck with arrows, his head low to the ground. He was still tense, growling as if he would attack. I pressed my hands against the crackling grass and pushed myself back, back, as hard and fast as I could, my wounded leg dragging on the ground. But he was faster.

He pounced, and I screamed my song again, just

one line, one rattled tune. His jaws snapped a hands-breadth from my face, his spittle flying against my lips. His breath stank of blood, and I couldn't seize enough breath to sing again. His maw opened toward my throat, but before he could clamp down, his body slumped. At last the weight of those arrows in him was too great. The full force of his body collapsed on me. He didn't move again.

I thought I was dead too. A hot pain pierced my ankle, a dull pain throbbed in my head. I was pinned to the ground by the wolf's corpse and surrounded by an angry anthill of soldiers. Chinua, his face full of rage and grief, ran forward and prodded his wolf lord to see if he was dead. I pushed against the hairy body with all my strength. The corpse rolled a little to the right, but it was so heavy, I couldn't budge it from my leg.

Then for whole moments, I heard no sound but my own heartbeat.

I let my head fall back, and I gazed into the Eternal Blue Sky. It was morning. Some of the sky was yellow, some the softest blue. One small cloud scuttled along. Strange how everything below can be such death and chaos and pain while above the sky is peace, sweet blue gentleness. I heard a shaman say once, the Ancestors want our souls to be like the blue sky.

I prayed to the sky—*Here I am. I took what the*

260

Ancestors gave me and I avenged their names. You saw it. You're above all, even the sun, even the Sacred Mountain, even the Ancestors. I submit to you, and if you're sending me on to see my mama again, I'm ready to go. Just take care of my lady, please, and Tegus, too.

And I closed my eyes to die. But you see that I'm not dead, as I'm still writing. Under heeded my pleas today, though he still tricked me in my turn.

The drums rapped and the horns called. I turned my head and saw five hundred warriors coming from the west gate of the city, Batu at their lead. They halted a safe distance from Khasar's men.

"My lady, are you all right?" Batu shouted to me.

"Yes," I said, because it seemed what he expected to hear. And I was alive still, which I guess was all right.

He gestured with his chin to the dead creature pinning me. "Is that Khasar?"

"It was."

"In wolf form, just as you said. Beware a lady's faith, you warriors of Under's Scorn."

Chinua looked made of wrath. A company of warriors had come forward, standing behind him with weapons in hand. "You should beware us, Evela's peasants! Carthen's Glory is not defeated by the slaying of one wolf."

Batu shrugged. "I have nearly thirty thousand

warriors ready at the gates, men fighting for their homes. Your numbers are larger, true, but with your wolf lord dead, how many will fight? He was your real strength. If you leave now, you'll make it home before true winter falls. Don't waste the time. Throw down your weapons, let us take Lady Saren safely away, and we won't pursue."

There was more talk, I think, but I didn't catch it. It took so much effort to try and listen. My ears were so frozen I wouldn't have been surprised to see them break right off my head. My feet seemed to have never existed at all, and my throat screamed with every inhale. Pressed against the ground like that, I was so cold, the only parts of me I could feel were throbbing something vicious, and I wanted to howl and cry with the pain, but I couldn't move enough to do that much.

Suddenly the ache in my ankle pierced me like a new wound, and I screamed before I realized what had happened. Chinua and two other warriors had rolled the wolf off me. They began to tow the carcass toward their camp, and behind them, Khasar's warriors retreated. I guess Batu had been pretty convincing.

I sat up and almost fainted from pain. I paused, waiting for the blackness in my vision to go away so I could stand, and I found myself looking into the eyes of the wolf. They were dragging him by his hind legs, and his dead eyes stared back at me. In death, his eyes lost their wildness. They calmed and saddened some, and I realized that his wolf eyes were as blue as the Eternal Sky. I wonder if right at the moment of his death, Khasar remembered the price his wolf strength cost. He offered his soul to the desert shamans. Now it can never climb the Sacred Mountain, never enter the Realm of the Ancestors. I suppose it's the path he chose. I suppose it's what he deserves.

"My lady," said Batu, "can you come to me?"

Chinua and his warriors had withdrawn, but I understood that Batu didn't dare turn his back on them, nor could he risk riding to me and putting any more distance between him and the path of retreat.

I nodded and stood on my left leg, making sure my cloak was tight around me. I couldn't feel its warmth.

I didn't know how I would walk. I hopped a few steps and felt ridiculous, a just-hatched bird, hobbling and unsure, while thousands of warriors watched me. So I thought I'd risk one step on my right foot. That was a mistake, I thought, as I yelped in pain and fell forward.

Suddenly one of Batu's soldiers was dismounting, running to my side. He lifted me under my knees and carried me back to his horse, boosting me up onto his saddle as if I weighed no more than a cat. His face was buried in a deep, fur-lined hood, and he rested a moment against his mare, bent forward as if he'd a pain in his middle. He groaned as he pulled himself into the saddle behind me, but he held me on his lap, one arm under my knees to keep my legs from bouncing against the horse. He wrapped his other arm around my waist as if to warm me as well as keep me on the saddle.

"My lord," I said as we rode back toward the city.

The horse's canter jostled my ankle and I couldn't help whimpering. The pain was like being stuck with a knife again, again, again.

Tegus held me tighter. "We've got to get you

inside city walls and out of bowshot, and then I'll ask Bloodnose here to give us a nice, smooth walk. Just a little farther, just hang on."

"I'm all right," I said, pretending I didn't have pain tears streaking down my face. And I was so cold, my teeth had begun to chatter like a hammer against my jaw. "I could keep riding . . . all day. Why don't we . . . go mushroom hunting?"

"Now that's a fine idea and I would agree, but I must admit I'm embarrassed to be out with such a scatterbrain. It seems, my lady, you forgot yet again to put on shoes this morning. What would your mother say?"

"I just wanted Khasar's opinion . . . on whether my ankles are . . . sturdier than yours."

"And what did he say?"

"I don't think he . . . liked my ankles so well. He fell on me . . . and broke one."

"That wasn't very kind," he agreed, talking lightly as if to distract me from the pain. "I think there are better ways to tell a person you don't approve of their ankles than to break them."

"That's what . . . I thought, too. His manners always were . . . la—lacking."

His arm held me tighter to him. "You're going to have to marry me now."

"But . . . I . . ."

"You slew Khasar, you healed me, and you have perfect ankles. I really don't think this is a question we need to debate."

"As always . . . my lord, you make perfect sense."

His cheek was next to mine. He pulled me closer, his warmth so wonderful, my skin stung against his touch. And he kissed my neck, behind my ear. Kissed me once, quietly.

So you see, I agreed. To marry Khan Tegus. As Lady Saren. Ancestors, my thoughts must've been as numb as my feet.

And now here I am in a chamber stacked with furs and silks, with a fire at both ends of the room and three large windows, ice covered in a soft cloth pressed to my swollen jaw, my broken ankle wrapped and resting on pillows. And everyone calling me Lady Saren.

The sticking-needle pain of my warming feet has passed. I should go to the kitchens and tell my lady. Tell her that her khan wants to wed her. And it's time for her to say who she is. And who I'm not.

I'll go tomorrow.

Day 165

Shria visited me this morning, smiling. She said the chiefs voted that although Lady Saren's betrothal to Khan Tegus wasn't sanctioned by her father, he's dead now so that matter is meaningless, and since our (their) betrothal came first, he'll marry me (Lady Saren) and not Lady Vachir.

Shria said, "It's complicated for a ruling lady of one realm to marry a ruling lord of another—usually that lot is left to younger siblings. And now that Khasar's war isn't an issue, Lady Vachir's advisers seemed relieved that the betrothal ties were released."

She seemed to be holding something back, so I asked, "How did Lady Vachir take it?"

Shria frowned, then patted my cheek. "Don't worry about that. Even if her pride is hurt, Lady Vachir can't cause you any trouble now that the chiefs have decided. You'll have your wedding day."

She handed me a note from Khan Tegus and left me to read it.

We've been betrothed for five years so it doesn't make sense to wait longer. We'll have the wedding in nine days. Now that the date's set, I won't come see you until our wedding day—because it's bad luck and because you might protest the haste. If you try to put it off, I'll have Batu argue with you, and he's very good at it. Rest your ankle. There will be dancing.

—Tegus

So it's real. It's happening. And I'm lost.

I went to look for Saren, hobbling out of my room with the help of two canes, when Tegus came down the hallway. When he saw me, he skipped a step. He looked to see if we were alone, picked me up, hurried around a corner, and kissed me. Kissed me long. My canes clattered to the floor, my arms fit around his neck. I felt as though my whole body only now was thawing. While he was holding me I forgot that I'm not who I say I am, that he doesn't know that I'm just Dashti. How can anyone forget? But I did. And I wish I hadn't remembered again.

When we stopped to breathe, he said, "I wanted to show you something," and pulled from his belt a blue shirt I remembered well.

"The one I gave you," I said.

"I kept it with me until your scent faded from the

fabric. I should have known you when you first came to sing for my leg, I should have remembered. . . ."

He pressed his cheek against mine. He breathed in against my neck and sighed deep inside. I closed my eyes. I tried to memorize the warm, brown, cinnamon smell of his skin. In case I never smell it again.

"Will you take your shirt?" he asked. "Will you wear it for me? Against your skin, so it carries your scent again."

"Yes, my lord," I whispered. "Yes, Tegus."

"Do you have a lady's maid with you? Would you like me to find you one?"

"No, I'd rather not have a maid. I'm fine."

"Are you? Have you warmed back up again?" He rubbed my arms.

"Yes, I have. I'm fine, really. Actually, I'm wonderful." Just then, I felt it.

"You are," he agreed. Then he kissed me again, saying, "Mmm," as though my lips tasted better than candied fruit. "Don't tell. The chiefs believe I won't see you until the wedding, and you know how rigorous those chiefs can be about tradition."

He set me gently down, fetched me my canes, then ran off.

I came back to my room and sat alone. I can't go see my lady right now, not until I can stop crying.

Later

When I made my way to the kitchens, I passed by Lady Vachir's open door. Since travel in the winter is uncomfortable, even deadly, she's staying in the khan's house until spring, the thought of which makes me want to scratch the spider tickles off my back. She and all her maids stared at me as I passed by. I'm feeling like an antelope without a herd, with hunters riding down the hill.

Cook let me talk to Saren, saying, "Yes, my lady," and "Certainly, my lady," eyeing my new clothes as though the yellow brocade was fresh meat and she was starving. Saren and I sat in the empty sugar closet and I explained it all to her, as simply as I could.

"I did what you asked, I did my duty, and he's proved himself true to you. The chiefs ruled in your favor, Lady Vachir's betrothal is no more, and your wedding date is set. Now is the time to tell him who you are."

She shook her head. "You marry him as me first, then he won't be able to change his mind. Once he takes the vows for Lady Saren —"

"But I'm not Lady Saren!"

"You'll be acting as me. They'll understand."

Ancestors, what have I done? I think I'd rather face Khasar again, naked on a winter battlefield, than marry Tegus as Lady Saren. Won't he feel betrayed? I wish I had someone to plead for advice, but I've sworn secrecy. Besides, if any discover I've claimed nobility, they could hang me just like Osol. I think I know what Lady Vachir would do—something involving removing my intestines while I still breathed. I've seen her eyes. I think she'd take pleasure in it.

Here in my room, I fold myself toward the Sacred Mountain for hours, praying, praying. Meanwhile, her lord's house is aflutter with wedding preparations. The poor girls in the kitchen must be drowning in dirty pots.

Day 167

The answer occurred to me early in the morning. I have to leave. My lady doesn't know what it is she's asking me to do, and I can't make her understand. Ancestors forgive me, but I can't dress in a marriage deel and pretend to be Lady Saren, take the vows to love her khan, and then step back for my lady. I can't make that lie, and I can't watch what will happen next.

Tegus, I'm leaving this book behind for you, so you will know the why of it all, and maybe you'll forgive me, or maybe you'll think me false and reprehensible. You'd be justified. I couldn't stand the thought of your reading all my words unless I knew for certain that I'd never have to face you again, so please don't look for me. If you read the book in its entirety, you'll know for truth who is Lady Saren. And I guess you'll also know that I'm a silly girl who writes down every word you said to me.

Please, Tegus, dress Saren in blue silk and let her hands be beautiful again. I think you'll worry for me because it's winter and I don't have a gher, but I'm a mucker and I'll find a way. Thank you. Forgive me. Don't worry.

I'll leave tomorrow.

Day 169

I thought I'd never write in this book again. I'm in yet another new room, though this one has no window, this one has a door that locks. It's underground, but it smells like the tower, and that smell makes my stomach spin and my vision dim and my skin itch as if ghost spiders cover me, and I scratch and scratch here in the dark. I'll be hanging before the week is out. But I'm trying not to think about that.

Yesterday I was too slow leaving, and I can't blame it all on my ankle. Why didn't I just get out into the city as quickly as I could hobble? I'm such a fool. And yet mostly what I feel right now is sad, all-out-of-food sad, lonely sad, sorry sad. Shamed sad, and hoping never to have to look Khan Tegus in the face again. And yet every moment hoping that he'll open that door. Why is that?

Yesterday I crept from my room early in the morning. I put on the blue shirt Tegus returned to me, my old wool deel, sheepskin cloak, and boots, forgetting my gloves in my hurry. I left this book behind for Tegus. When I passed Lady Vachir's room, her door was open and she watched me walk by.

My thought was to join the refugees in the streets. If I took the seven years' vow of servitude, maybe someone would take me in. I hoped to find a family who planned to leave Song for Evela come spring so I could disappear from the city as soon as I might.

My mistake was stopping in the kitchen. I'd thought it too cruel not to explain things to Saren and say good-bye to Qacha and Gal. I found the two girls scrubbing pots, and I sneaked in to work beside them a last time, whispering as we washed.

"I can't tell you why I lied, but I think rumors will bring it to your ears soon enough."

They didn't press, though they seemed sorry to have me go. I thought Qacha would miss me as much as I'd miss her, and poor Gal had heartbreak in her eyes.

"I liked thinking that you'd been gentry all along," Gal said, "that you were going to be the khan's bride. And if your story isn't true, then what about . . . well, how can anything impossible actually happen?"

I knew she was thinking of her family, if they were alive, if they would find their way to Song for Evela. I said, "If they come for you, it'll most likely be in the spring." I didn't have a better answer.

My lady didn't take the news as kindly. We sat in the empty sugar closet. I closed the door when she began to yell.

"I order you to stay! I order you to marry him in my name. By the sacred nine, Dashti, you'll do what I say."

Strangely, her words held no sway over me. Maybe it's wrong, but I don't think I have to do what she says just because I'm a mucker and she's an honored lady. I smiled to myself then, thinking that if I were in a tower now and a black-gauntleted Khasar told me to put my hand back down so he could slap it, I'd tell him to go slap himself.

"No, my lady," I said as gently as I could. "I've tried to do my duty by you, but I won't do this."

Then she struck my face, just like her father and Lady Vachir, too. This time I didn't laugh. I just stood up slowly. Her eyes went wide, and I think she was afraid I'd hit her back. Not to say that I wasn't tempted.

"I'm sorry, my lady," I said. "My Lord the cat is a better companion for you than I am anyway."

My lady didn't cry, though her chin set to quivering. "Don't abandon me, Dashti. Everyone does, but you don't, you never do."

Those words pinched my heart. Poor little lost lamb, poor thin and wind-tossed thing.

"Oh Saren." I sat beside her and she put her head on my shoulder and lost every inch of the slapping, commanding gentry. "I could take you with me, but you really are better off here than living like a mucker. Khan Tegus is a good man, the best of men, the very best. He'll take care of you." I held her hands, I smiled to show her my confidence, and I felt as much like a good mucker mama as I ever hope to. "You've done so well these past weeks. I think you can be strong without me. This is your time, Saren. This is your chance to be brave. Stand up. Declare who you are. Will you do it?"

She hesitated. "I'll try. I'll think about it."

I left then. I should've gone straight out, hidden my mottled face beneath my hood, and lost myself in the city, but I slowed to say good-bye to Mucker. Fool, fool, fool. The yak would've been fine without a farewell, but now I am not.

When I emerged from the stable, Lady Vachir was in the kitchen yard, and with her the three vulture maids and a dozen warriors from Beloved of Ris. In her right hand, she was clutching this book.

I turned and fled. The ground was thick with ice. I could hear them shouting. I didn't look, I just hobbled toward the gate. I was nearly there when my canes slipped and my feet flew out from under me. I was on the ground, and when I looked up, warriors from Beloved of Ris surrounded me.

I screamed, I couldn't help it. Hands were on my arms and legs, pulling me to a chopping block in the center of the yard, and they were none too gentle with my broken ankle. One stood by, ready with a sword. I screamed louder and thrashed and kicked with my good leg. Everyone working in the yard stared, but no one moved to interfere with Lady Vachir's business.

The girls emerged from the kitchens, shivering without cloaks but too curious about the commotion not to peek. When they recognized me in the hands of the warriors, they ran forward. All except Saren, who went back inside.

"What are you doing?" Cook hollered, running at them with a kitchen knife. "Put Lady Saren down, you mangy villains!"

"This isn't Lady Saren." Lady Vachir spoke loudly enough for any bystander to hear. "This is Dashti the mucker maid. Isn't that right?"

If ever there was a good time to lie, that would've been it. But there we were, under the Eternal Blue Sky, and I just couldn't do it. Cook frowned at my silence and took a step back.

"By the ancient law of the Ancestors," said Lady Vachir, "it's my right to take the life of anyone who interferes with my lawful betrothal. This girl isn't Lady Saren, she isn't a lady at all. She's a commoner, a mucker from Titor's Garden, and confessed the truth herself in this book."

Gal and Qacha were beside us now, tugging on the warriors' sleeves, pushing their way to me. The warriors didn't strike the girls, just shoved and wriggled them off their arms. My head lay on the chunk of wood where fowl get their necks chopped. It was stained muddy red and colder than ice, and with my last thought I felt some real sympathy for those poor chickens.

The warriors had dragged Gal out of the way. Now only Qacha stood between me and the sword.

"You can't just kill her!" said Qacha. "Can they?"

"No, not until the khan's chiefs rule it so!" Gal shouted.

The warriors hesitated. Lady Vachir scowled. Apparently she knew that Gal was right.

"Then cut off one of her feet," said the lady, "so she can't run away again."

At those words, my ankles flamed with pain.

The warriors rolled me around until my broken and wrapped ankle lay on the chopping block. Maybe they figured it was already damaged and so not such a tragedy. I tried to kick with my left leg until someone pinned it to the ground. I screamed and fought, but I couldn't move.

The sword rose above me. I looked up at it, silver against blue sky, and I was a fool enough to think, *Isn't that pretty? Silver on blue.* I held my breath while I waited for the blade to drop. I didn't look down, I didn't want to see blood, see my leg end at my ankle. I just kept staring up and thinking, *silver on blue, silver on blue.*

I hadn't realized that the girls had been screaming until they stopped. The sword quivered and didn't fall.

The hands holding me let go, and I thumped onto the ground. I wiggled my toes. All ten were still there.

Khan Tegus was crouching beside me, short of breath. I could see Saren standing behind him, her cheeks pink from running.

"I got him," she said, proud as a rooster. "I found him, Dashti. I was brave."

Tegus scooped my hands into his. The mist of his breath wrapped around my face, and he spoke to me as though we were all alone. "Ancestors, your hands are cold. First I find you bootless on a battlefield, now with your feet on a chopping block. And with bare hands, no less."

"Hello," was all I could manage back.

"Are you hurt?" he asked, and though his voice was gentle toward me, I sensed anger in it. He wasn't angry at me then, but I knew he would be soon.

"Alive still," I said, "and with both my feet intact even."

There's something about being with Tegus that feels like privacy. The way he looks at me or touches me, we can be in a room full of people but I always feel as though we're alone, no one else in the world. I felt that way then, his white breath and mine mingling, his large hands trying to warm my own.

But then Lady Vachir spoke up. Of course she would.

"My lord, that girl is not Lady Saren."

He helped me to my feet, and I wobbled on one leg, so he put an arm around my waist to hold me steady. The shouting and explaining and accusing had started again, but I didn't hear much of it. My head felt as though it were still pressed to the block, and everyone was talking at once, and I was watching Tegus, the anger in his eyes, the doubt creasing his forehead. All I could think was, *When will he let go of me?* That wondering was bigger than my head.

"Enough!" Tegus shouted. He turned to me. "Is it true, what she says she read?"

"My name's Dashti," I said, as simply as I could. I knew it was all about to end and I didn't want to lie anymore. "I'm not Lady Saren. I'm a mucker maid, no more." I wouldn't point out the real Saren now, not with Lady Vachir there hoping for someone to chop up.

He asked Lady Vachir for my book. She gripped it.

"Lady Vachir," he said quietly, "stealing is also a crime."

She placed it in his hands, her expression carefully casual. He pressed it back into mine.

"Keep this close to you," he whispered.

Then, at last, came the moment when his arm fell away from my waist. I shivered as he took a step back, suddenly as frozen inside as out. Perhaps it's irony that I'd met Khasar naked on the battlefield, but I felt colder now.

After he let me go, warriors carried me here, locked me in. I stared at my one candle for hours. I couldn't bear to look away.

This evening Shria brought some supper, and with it my horsehair blanket, some ink, and a brush. She didn't speak to me, but she touched my cheek before she left. I tore a blank page out of this book and thought to write Tegus an explanation. I crossed out the words again and again before I gave up. Every word I write to him sounds false. I can't speak the whole truth—that I wasn't only acting out of duty for my lady, how it was my own shirt I gave him. How parts of me wanted to be his lady, just for a moment even.

Stop it, Dashti. None of that matters now. My whole, heavy world hangs by a thin rope. I remember a time when I comprehended Saren's plea to die, but not now. Now I want to live. Ancestors, please, I want to keep on living.

It's cold down here.

Day 170

Khan Tegus came this morning. He asked me again if it was all true.

"Yes," I said.

He groaned and paced. I didn't explain. I guess I always knew it would come to this, and trying to change it now seemed like trying to stop the wind from blowing across the steppes. Besides, the excuse "my lady ordered me to" sounded so feeble in my head. She ordered me, but I chose to obey.

"Lady Vachir is claiming blood rights," he said. "Protection of binding betrothals is as old as cities, since the days men would get brides by kidnapping. The law is severe on that point, and my chiefs say she's within the law, and . . . Dashti, I don't know what to do."

"Have you spoken with Lady Saren?"

He looked sharply at me. "Is she Lady Saren? She's been claiming such, and I told her to be quiet about it and stay hidden in the kitchens. No need to give Vachir another target."

"If it comes to dying" — I sat on my hands so he couldn't see them shake — "if it comes to that, don't be anxious for me. I have a mama in the Ancestors' Realm. She'll sing me in. I'll be all right."

I didn't want to say that. I wanted to throw myself on my knees and beg to keep breathing, but I can't have him breaking his heart for worrying about me. Even so, my words didn't seem to relieve him any. He put his face in his hands and breathed slowly for a long while. I think he might've cried, if he'd let himself. He might've cried for me. What a powerful thought.

"You're our champion." He let his hands drop. "You went out alone, you took down Khasar. But now Lady Vachir has made certain there's not a soul in this city who doesn't also know that you lied, you claimed to be gentry, you . . ." He sat beside me and was quiet for a while. I kept my eyes on his hands until he spoke again.

"Lady Saren's father visited Song for Evela when I was eight. I remember at a banquet, my father pulling me in close and saying, in almost a teasing way, 'He has a daughter named Saren. You might marry her one day, you know. What do you think about that?' When I was fourteen and received her first letter, it didn't seem strange because I'd had her in my mind all those years."

"You were meant to marry her," I said.

He shrugged. "The letters were a game. I was

young, I felt as though I were playing at being in love. I read poetry to try to learn how one courts with words, and I failed at it miserably. But it was fun, anticipating a new letter, hiding it from my father and hers, and we kept it up for a few years. When my father died before declaring who he wanted me to marry, I realized I might actually wed Lady Saren. I looked over her letters again, and I saw them anew—they were simple, little humor or life. To tell the truth, I was apprehensive at best. And then came news of the tower.

"I felt responsible, but I was dreading the meeting, too. It was you, wasn't it, Dashti? You were the one who spoke to me."

I nodded. I was wrapped up in the weave of his story and didn't want to speak.

"Of course it was you. I never should've left you in there. I should've risked war with Titor's Garden and Thoughts of Under. We met war anyway. When I spoke with Lady Saren in the tower, with you, it was a wonder. It felt right." He smiled. "Then I met you as Dashti, but when you told me you were Lady Saren, that felt right, too. And all has seemed right until . . . Ancestors, it's all wrong. You weren't Lady Saren in the tower, you weren't when you faced Khasar, you're not now and you won't ever be, and for that the chief of order says you must hang."

I thought I'd prepared myself for that end, but hearing him say it made my heart sting.

He rubbed his face again. "Dashti, I don't know what to do. I don't know. Can you, will you sing for me?"

So I sang him the song for clear thoughts, and after a time he leaned back against the wall with me and rested his head against mine, humming along. It was strange, as I think back on it now, that I'm the one scheduled to die but I was comforting him. At the time, it felt just right. It was a moment of peace, and it gave me space to think. We were betrothed once. I always knew it was ill-fated, but he truly believed I would be his bride. I guess I'd never realized that before. He had taken my mucker hand and looked at my mottled face and believed we would wed. And he hadn't seemed sorry. In fact, he'd swooped me up in the corridor and kissed me.

That set me to crying. He sat up and took my hand, the one mottled, holding it to his lips.

"Dashti, oh Dashti, I'm sorry." He smoothed my hair against the back of my head, he held my forehead to his. "Please, I'm so sorry. Listen, nothing's settled yet. The chiefs may vote to preserve your life.

A lesser sentence might be banishment from Song for Evela."

Ancestors know that I never would've said aloud what I thought then—that living didn't matter to me if it meant I'd be alone, that I'd have to leave Tegus behind. Is that silly? And yet I really feel it. Here's what I wished I could say—*Tegus, I'll not find a better man than you, not on the steppes, not in any city or in all the wilds of the Eight Realms. You're better than seven years of food. You're better than windows. You're even better than the sky.*

But I couldn't tell him that, and since I had to hold back words, I wanted to give him something. "Take my book of thought keeping," I said. "It's all I have that I care about."

"Haven't you destroyed it yet? I gave it back to you so you could. It's the best evidence against you." He put it back in my hands and stood at once. Before he passed through my door, he turned and said, "I'm sorry, Dashti."

And I guess that's the last time I'll ever see him.

After he left, I sat on the ground and stared at the door for a long time. A very long time. I didn't want to move ever again. Eventually I got myself up so I could write what Tegus said. To keep telling my story seems like the last bit of living I can still do. I feel like a dragonfly clinging to a grass blade in a windstorm, but I can't just let go. I can't. I stare at the candle, how the flame shivers and bends when the wick is too long. The light is small and unsteady, but unless it's snuffed out, it'll keep burning for as long as the wick runs.

There's a stinging, cold sensation that shivers through my blood. I look at my hands, stare at how they're shaking, and wonder if this is how Osol felt the night before he died. I wonder if everyone who faces death hurts like this. It's as though for the first time I realize how much just being alive makes my body ache. But I don't want that ache to stop.

Day 171

What a long, cold night it was. I guess I can admit that I wept instead of sleeping. Odd how much that made my throat hurt. With no window, no way to track the time, I felt as though I spent days here alone. When Shria came with breakfast, she assured me that it was just barely morning out in the world. Along with cheese and bread, she brought news.

"There's quite a tumult in your kitchens," she said. "The family of one of the girls made it out of Goda's Second Gift and came here. Seems it was pretty rough going, traveling into winter, but they didn't stop until they found their daughter."

"Gal," I said. A grin took over my face and felt like an old friend come home.

The news changed me, and I've been thinking and buzzing for hours. Though the only light I have is a candle and even wrapped up in my blanket my bones are cold like stones, I'm filled with a kind of wonder, I guess. A wonder that burns. If Gal's family is alive and found her, if her impossible wish came true, what else can happen? It makes me almost believe that everything works out somehow, and even if the best possible ending for all this is for me to speedily join my mama in the Realm of the Ancestors, then so be it. That is an ending to be proud of.

And I've decided a second thing—I don't care if this book is evidence against me. I've thought and thought and folded myself toward the Sacred Mountain and prayed to all the Ancestors, and what I know is that I'm tired of deception and lies. I want Tegus to know all. Even if it be my end. Endings aren't so bad. After the night I endured, any ending sounds like peace.

When Shria returns, I'll send this book with her to the khan. The thought of him reading these silly thoughts of mine makes me want to pull the horsehair blanket over my head. But so be it. I am done. Besides, if I'm being truly honest, I must admit that ever since I first heard his voice outside the tower, I've been writing this book for him. To him. It's his more than mine.

And whoever reads this, be it Tegus or Shria or anyone, I've kept my wages in the far left corner of the sugar closet beneath the pile of empty sacks. I wish you'd give them to Gal's family to get them started. I hate to think of those coins lying idle and doing no good.

Day 174

This book of thought keeping must have the soul of a good mare who always returns to her master, for here it is, in my hands again. I have much to tell and little time, so here I go.

After I last wrote, Shria came again to my locked room, bringing supper, and I sent her away with this book in hand and a request to give it to Khan Tegus. I waited two more days, knowing nothing. No one came but a kitchen boy whose name I never learned, bringing raisin rice, carrot salad, and milk to drink. No meat for prisoners. That's the law.

Those two days felt as long as a tower year. I've grown accustomed to easing loneliness and worry by writing my thoughts here or making a sketch of what I see. Being alone, without even this book to write in—well, I guess that's about as lonely as I've ever felt. I began to imagine that the world had swallowed me and I was lost and trapped deep in its belly with . . . never mind, I don't want to think about it anymore.

After two days Shria returned. Her mouth was wrinkled like a winter carrot as she frowned at me— she wasn't angry, more sorry.

"Say prayers if you wish, Dashti," she said. "You won't be coming back here. Whatever fate they decide for you, they'll enact it today."

I said prayers. I didn't know what to pray for, so instead I just folded myself toward the north and, closing my eyes, tried to fill myself with memories of the Eternal Blue Sky. How can a body be too sad or frightened or lonely when she's filled up her soul with the highest sky blue? I left my horsehair blanket behind but told Shria that if they were to hang me, I wouldn't mind my body being covered in that brown blanket. It's been a good comfort to me. She nodded. I think she was too teary to speak. Ancestors bless her.

Then upstairs to the large feasting hall. Lady Vachir was there, the seven chiefs of Song for Evela and one empty chair, four shaman, my lady, and Khan Tegus. I hadn't realized that he'd be there. Everyone was frowning at me.

The city chief, a squat woman with black eyes, led the tribunal. "We're here to decide the fate of Dashti, a lady's maid, who claimed nobility and betrothal to our khan."

It was the chief of order's responsibility to lay out my crimes, and she did a very good job. While she spoke, she held this book in her hand, and I guessed that before Shria was able to deliver it to the khan, the chief of order had taken a look.

"Dashti," she said. She had a very tiny mouth. It unnerved me. "Dashti, why did you claim to be Lady Saren?"

"My lady asked me to," I said. "She ordered me on the sacred nine, and I had sworn to obey her."

"Hmm," said the chief. Then she opened this book and began to read parts aloud, parts that made me wish I could bury myself alive. How I gave Tegus my own shirt, when I said my lady smelled like hot dung, when I said I hated her, when I described the smell of Tegus's neck . . . Ancestors, it was horrible to hear. Every word made me hate myself more, and I decided that they'd be right to hang me.

"Do you have any defense for yourself, Dashti?" asked the chief of order.

I didn't. I couldn't think of anything, and I couldn't bear to look at Tegus. At that moment, my one wish was for a rope around my neck as fast as possible.

"Then I demand her blood!" Lady Vachir arose and began to shout for my death, and not by hanging but my head on the chopping block so my blood would be spilled. That bit seemed to go on forever, and I thought, *I really am going to die today. And the end is just and everything will be fine.*

While they shouted, I concentrated on sitting up straight. My thoughts kept returning to the idea of silver on blue, silver on blue. Oddly enough, that image of the sword against the sky was comforting to me. Maybe because the sword never fell?

And then the khan stood, calming Lady Vachir back into her seat.

"Since Dashti doesn't give her own defense, chiefs, I ask for the right to do so for her."

The chiefs nodded. The khan approached my chair, and I kept my eyes on his boots.

"First, allow me to examine other entries." He opened the book and read some from times in the tower, when I didn't want to speak for Saren, when I worried and prayed, when I begged her not to order me to. He read the entire entry from the day I gave My Lord the cat to Saren. He read my encounter with Khasar. There were murmurs of approval from some of the chiefs then.

"There was another part that caught my interest as well," said the khan. "The day you arrived in Song for Evela. First, Dashti, you are a mucker, is that correct?"

"Yes, my lord."

"Forgive our ignorance of mucker ways, but as more folk from the steppes come here, we're beginning to learn. I understand that, according to the law of the steppes, if a mucker offers her last animal to another family or clan, accepting that gift means recognizing the mucker as a member of the family. Is that so?"

I guess I just gaped at him then, I was so confused. What in all the realms was he saying? And when was he going to condemn me to death?

"Shria, please relate your first encounter with Dashti."

The white-haired woman stood. "She arrived at the gates with Lady Saren and a brown yak. She said she wanted to give the yak to Khan Tegus, that it was a gift for him."

"Did she ask payment?"

"No, in fact the gatekeeper stated no payment would be given, and she offered it anyway."

"Did she trade the animal in return for employment?"

"No, she gave the animal freely. I offered her scrubber work after the gift had been given."

The khan nodded, satisfied. "I submit to you, chiefs, that Dashti presented me with her last animal, her only means of livelihood, and as such has the right to expect family status. I formally accept her gift of . . . ," he turned to me, "a yak, was it?"

"Yes, a very fine yak," I said. For he is—the finest yak I've ever known.

The khan nodded. "Of a very fine yak. Here's where two laws collide, chiefs. Do we honor Lady Vachir's claim of blood against any who threaten her betrothal? Or do we protect Dashti as a member of my own family?"

Lady Vachir stood. "Chiefs, I demand—"

"Wait, please, my lady, wait a little longer before getting back to the demands. I recognize that this argument isn't enough to stay your claim to blood right, but there is more. Lady Saren?"

He took Saren's hand to help her rise from her seat, and I thought, *That's how they'll hold hands when they're wed.*

"This is the true Lady Saren of Titor's Garden. I have her letters here," he placed parchments on the table before the chiefs, "accepting my offer of betrothal."

"My lord," said the chief of order, "we've already ruled that your betrothal to Lady Saren precedes that to Lady Vachir. You have every right to marry the true Lady Saren, but this doesn't excuse Dashti's crimes."

"Lady Saren," asked the khan, all business. "Why did Dashti claim she was you?"

"I ordered her to. I told her to act in my name." She turned to Lady Vachir and said, "It was my right," offering along with the words a very convincing glare.

The chief of animals shook her head. "Acting for her lady is the duty of a lady's maid, but professing to be her? Claiming her name? No. We're hearing reasons for the behavior but nothing that pardons the maid. Pretending nobility is the grossest crime imaginable."

"Grosser than trading the soul's freedom to the desert shamans?" Batu said in a grumble that didn't carry far beyond the chief's table. "Grosser than razing Titor's Garden?"

All were quiet for a moment. Then the chief of animals spoke again.

"Nevertheless, the law is paramount. If we don't obey the law, then we create as much chaos as Khasar and his army. If I had to vote now —"

"A moment, chief, please, I beg you. Don't cast your vote just yet." Khan Tegus turned back to Saren. "My lady, tell me what you told me this morning."

Saren smiled, dimples and all, and didn't even clutch her own hands as she said, "Dashti is my sister."

I started to gasp but choked on it.

"Now let's be clear," said Tegus. "Has she always been your sister?"

"No." Saren was smiling fit to split her face in half. Her voice clipped in such a way that I guessed she'd rehearsed this answer and was proud to be getting it right. "But she stayed with me when everyone else left. And . . . and we spent nearly three years locked in a tower, and when we came out, it was as though we were birth . . . uh, being born anew. All my real family was dead."

"How did they die?"

"Killed by Lord Khasar. And then Dashti faced him and helped av—aveg . . ."

"Avenge," said the khan.

"Avenge my family and defend my honor." She looked at me, hard, and then she straightened up, turned herself toward the chiefs, and said in as bold a voice as I've ever heard, "Hear me, chiefs, the last lady of Titor's Garden. Dashti never betrayed me, never abandoned me. She was as true a lady's maid as the Ancestors ever created."

There was power in her voice, and the chiefs took notice. How could they not? I've seen my lady begin to change since the cat purred in her lap, since she found use for her hands in the kitchen, since Khasar died, but never until that moment had she looked like I thought gentry should. Like anyone should. More than a thousand days we've been together, more than a thousand songs I've sung for her, and only now, I think, do I see Saren truly begin to heal.

"And since I have no more family," Saren said, "it's my right under the Ancestors to declare Dashti my sister and an honored daughter of Titor's Garden."

I think that's the part where I did gasp and gulp at the same time, which set me coughing.

"Oh, one more question for Shria," said the khan. "Please tell the chiefs what you told me before, what you found in Dashti's room after she fled this house, the day Lady Vachir's warriors tried to cut off her foot."

Shria cleared her throat. "Nothing, my lord. I mean, everything. That room was filled with silk and brocade deels, silver and porcelain bowls and cups, hair combs decorated with pearls. She left them all behind, only took her old clothing, the very rags she'd been wearing when she arrived." She looked at the chiefs. "Seemed to me that if she were lying about who she was for selfish reasons, she would've taken some of those nice things to sell out in the city."

"Thank you, Shria." He turned to the chiefs. "I submit to you Dashti, a mucker maid. She said she was gentry, but is that a crime for one who was named as a sister by the lady of Titor's Garden, or for one who earned the right to be considered a member of my own honored family? She proved herself loyal to her lady even unto risking her own life, an act that should far outweigh any impropriety. As well, she faced Khasar alone on the battlefield and, blessed by the Ancestors themselves, walked away from it, victorious. For my vote, one in the nine, I find her actions justified, and what some would call a crime, I declare a noble act of loyalty. How find you?"

There was a horrible silence as the chiefs thought, some whispering to one another, some shaking their heads. Khan Tegus clenched his jaw and his eyes were fearful. I knew it would take just four chiefs to find me guilty. It is assumed that the chief in the empty chair will always vote for death.

The oldest chief, the one who serves Evela, goddess of sunlight, turned to the four shamans and asked, "What say you, holy ones?"

The shaman who'd read the sheep bones and declared Khasar couldn't be defeated by strength looked at me when he spoke. "I haven't read the signs or submitted to a trance, but my instinct says the Ancestors love this girl."

"Hmm," said the chief. And again, the horrible silence, which was finally broken by Batu, who hit his palm against the table, making everyone jump.

"Come now, my friends. This isn't so difficult. Our khan has done a mightier job here than even we dull-brained lot needed. Who among you really thinks this girl committed a crime?"

Several chiefs shook their heads, a couple squirmed, but not one raised a fist to vote. The mood exhaled. I think I might've cried.

"Disgraceful," said Lady Vachir, as she and all her vulture maids marched out of the room. Winter or not, I doubt Lady Vachir will be staying long in Song for Evela.

As soon as she was gone, Khan Tegus leaned against the table and sighed for relief so loudly, several people laughed. I didn't. I still couldn't breathe right.

"Thank the Ancestors," he said. "And you as well, honored chiefs. Thank you."

Saren embraced me. She did it clumsily, placing one arm around my neck and resting her head on my shoulder. She whispered, "I was scared, Dashti. I was really scared. I thought you might die and I really, really didn't want you to."

"You did well," I whispered back. "You spoke up like a lady. You were so brave." It made my eyes sting to say it, I really did feel as proud as any mucker mama. "Thank you, my lady."

She looked at me now and said, "No more 'my lady,' Dashti. No more of that."

I couldn't respond. I didn't know what to say. No

chance my mouth was going to let me call her sister. Not yet.

Batu was slapping Tegus on the back and laughing with relief. All the chiefs were standing, talking. A few were a bit disgruntled, but most seemed happy, excited even.

"And now at last," said the chief of light, "we'll have our khan's wedding. Lady Saren, may I be the first to congratulate you."

Tegus and Saren looked at each other. The whole room quieted. And I found reason to be glad I was still sitting.

Of course this is how it'll end, I told myself. This is how it should end. She's an honored lady. Isn't this what I've wanted for her? And I'll stay with her still and be her friend and coddle her babies, their babies, and keep my thoughts to myself and the pages of my book. It'll be all right. Saren will be the lady of Song for Evela and maybe I can write letters for her, advise her on things, be useful. It won't be so bad. It's an ending.

And though I reminded myself that I was just happy to be alive, some part of me wanted to shrink and die.

Tegus glanced at me once before saying, "Lady Saren, we *are* betrothed. Do you wish to wed me?"

Saren was watching me, and her eyes seemed troubled, but I can't be sure about that, because I felt like I was falling through the floor and seeing her from so far away.

"I'm not sure —," she started before the chief of order rushed forward and shushed everyone.

"My lord, may I hastily remind you that if you and Lady Saren break your betrothal, Lady Vachir will have full claim on your hand."

"Thank you, honored chief," said Tegus. "But Saren and I spoke this morning, and we both felt —"

"Careful," said the town chief, her eyes on the door. "I wouldn't advise you to say anything."

Saren was still looking at me when she said, "Then I will say." She drew herself up tall. "Khan Tegus, I would rather not marry you. However . . . ," she said loudly, cutting through the outcries from the chiefs, "however, I retain my right to our betrothal, and I exact it for my sister, Dashti."

Batu chuckled. Why was he laughing? Was it a joke on me?

Tegus didn't seem surprised. He offered Saren his hands, palms down. She took them, and he kissed her forehead as he would a younger sister.

Then he smiled at me, and I knew it wasn't a joke. Tegus would never play a cruel trick on me, and he never smiles by accident. He means each one. Then he was beside me. Then he was on one knee and taking my hand. And it felt like the tower, after he'd given me My Lord the cat when he held my hand, and everything in the world was inside that touch. And only the Ancestors know why, but I stopped feeling dizzy and confused, and all I wanted to do was laugh. So I did. Tegus did too, a surprised laugh.

"All right, all right," he said, forcing a straight face. "Here I go." He took a deep breath. "Dashti of Titor's Garden, Dashti of the steppes, will you please be my betrothed and my bride and my wife in this realm and the next?"

At those words, all laughter left me. Now, I've trembled before in steppes cold that's fit to freeze a yak. But when Tegus spoke those words, my arms took to shaking like I've never seen, and my legs knocking, my knees chattering, my whole body consumed to shivering so that I was afraid I couldn't keep my seat. I think I was crying too, and I wished I could leap up and dance, but it was all so much, my body couldn't hold it in. I shook and shook, my voice lost in the shudders.

So I looked to my lady. After all, I figured it was her turn to speak for me.

And Saren, understanding precisely what I wanted of her, faced Tegus and said, "Yes. She will."

Day 178

Today Tegus and I were wed, and Ancestors, but there was so much food! I wore a deel dyed as blue as the Eternal Sky, embroidered with yellow and gold thread, sunrise and sunset running up and down my sleeves. Qacha and Gal helped me dress and cooed over me as if I were the prettiest bride anyone had ever seen. Truth is, I felt it. I tried to wear a veil, but Tegus wouldn't have it.

"I want to see you as we take the vows. I want everyone to see you. My Dashti."

Then he kissed me on the mouth, though there were five chiefs in the room. Kissing like that in front of others may not be proper, but I felt certain that even the Ancestors didn't mind. I put my arms around his neck and kissed him back. Can a person actually float away from happiness?

A thing of wonder happened as Tegus and I took the vows. It was as though I'd been standing on one side of the room and suddenly everything swooped around and changed places, though nothing actually moved. It sounds strange, I know, but I felt the whooshing feeling in my belly, as if I were riding a mare that leaped from standing right into a gallop. And what caused that feeling inside me was this thought—I'm not a mucker marrying a khan. I'm Dashti marrying Tegus. And that feels just right. How Mama would laugh.

At the feast, Saren showed me all the trays of food she helped prepare. She doesn't have to work in the kitchens anymore, she has her own room and two sweet-voiced maids to call on for anything. But she likes to work with food, she says, and she likes to arrange things and make them look pretty. She looked more than pretty in a peach silk deel tonight, her hair in eight braids twisted up. Two of Tegus's cousins held a mock sword battle with tiny fish bones to see who got to sit beside her. I guess I've never heard her giggle so much. It *was* pretty funny, actually, and they do seem like decent boys, but I told Tegus no one has permission to court her until I know every detail of his life and personality. Saren deserves a gentle man, someone sweet who makes her laugh, who doesn't make her feel dull-witted, and when his arms are around her, she knows she's in the safest place in all the realms. We'll find the right one. Tegus has thirty-seven cousins.

There's still more feasting to be done and dancing

until the sun sets, and Tegus swore he could hold me as we danced so my injured leg would never touch the floor. I can hear the music just starting, but I hopped back here to our rooms so I could change my clothes.

During the tediously long ceremony, I was remembering when Tegus and I spoke through the tower and he'd said, "Would that I could take you out of here, and hold a feast and a dance, and see you bedecked in a silver deel." And there just happens to be a deel in the wardrobe made of silver silk. I can't wait to see his face when he sees me in it. I plan to laugh and laugh and dance and maybe I'll kiss him again, kiss my khan, right in front of the whole world.

ACKNOWLEDGMENTS

This book is based on the fairy tale "Maid Maleen," as recorded by the Grimm brothers, though I took many liberties with the original in my quest to find Dashti's story. Although I invented the Eight Realms, the setting was inspired in part by medieval Mongolia. Jack Weatherford's *Genghis Khan and the Making of the Modern World* was a fascinating read and huge help. Special thanks to Burd Jadamba, Sarantuya Batbold, Ariunaa Buyantogtokh, and Bonnie Bryner for the many stories and facts about Mongolia.

In researching and writing this story, I was impressed by the lifesaving difference one animal can make in a family's survival. We've been able to donate some of the proceeds of this book to Heifer International, an organization that gives important domestic animals to families in third world countries. Check out www.heifer.org, where you can donate a goat or water buffalo or flock of geese to a family in need.

As always, much credit goes to Victoria Wells Arms and Dean "The Family Yak" Hale for being inspired editors and readers, and to Max, for making the whole world new.

Kelly Sansom

SHANNON HALE

is the Newbery Honor–winning author of *Princess Academy*, *Book of a Thousand Days*, and the highly acclaimed and award-winning Books of Bayern: *The Goose Girl*, *Enna Burning*, *River Secrets*, and *Forest Born*. She has also written two novels for adults, *Austenland* and *The Actor and the Housewife*, and two graphic novels with her husband, *Rapunzel's Revenge* and *Calamity Jack*. She lives with her husband and two young children near Salt Lake City, Utah.

Visit Shannon on the Web for more information about all of her books: www.shannonhale.com

Book of a Thousand Days

Reading Group Guide

1. Did your feelings about Lady Saren change over the course of the book? Did you like her more or less after they escaped the tower? After they started working in the kitchen? When Saren ordered Dashti to stay with her? What do you think brought about the changes in Lady Saren over the course of the book?

2. "'You can tell something about a woman by what she names her children,'" Dashti says to Tegus right before they talk about what their names mean (page 183). Does your name have a special meaning? Do you know why your parents chose your name? Have you ever been teased about your name as Dashti and Tegus were?

3. At the beginning of the book, Dashti describes herself as simply "a mucker and a lady's maid," but by the end of the story she has become so much more. When Lady Saren orders her to stay, Dashti muses to herself, "Strangely, her words held no sway over me. Maybe it's wrong, but I don't think I have to do what she says just because I'm a mucker and she's an honored lady" (page 274). What do you think has brought about these changes in her? What words would you use to describe Dashti?

4. The color blue appears several times in the story: we read about the Eternal Blue Sky and the blue deel Dashti gives

to Tegus when she is in the tower, and when Lady Vachir is about to have Dashti's foot cut off for lying, Dashti thinks to herself repeatedly, "Silver on blue, silver on blue" (page 278). Can you think of other examples in the book where the color blue appears? Why do you think the color blue appears so many times in this story and what do you think it represents?

5. Dashti treasures My Lord the cat that Tegus gave to her in the tower, even though he thought he was giving it to Lady Saren. When the cat disappears, Dashti is very upset. Why do you think the cat is so important to Dashti? What do you think the cat symbolizes?

6. How did you feel when Dashti sang to My Lord to get him to be loyal to Lady Saren instead?

7. How does the way Dashti thinks of and interacts with gentry change over the course of the story? What do you think brings about this change?

8. The mucker songs have been passed down to Dashti from her mother. What are some objects or traditions in your family that have been passed down from one generation to another?

9. Dashti tries to bring about the marriage of Lady Saren to Lord Tegus, even though she obviously loves Tegus herself; do you think this makes her brave and loyal or foolish and too meek? Why?

10. If you were to produce a movie of *Book of a Thousand Days*, who would you cast in each role?

pring gusted into summer, and every day Rin ran. She ran over pine needles that snapped and moss that hushed. She zigzagged and changed paths, bolted through sunny clearings and back into cool shade. She sweated to exhale the tightness in her chest, to hide from a world that felt crowded, hostile, and too dense to breathe.

The exertion helped some, but today guilt cut her run short—Ma had need of her, and her brothers and their wives too. She took one look toward the deep Forest, longing to test its promise that she might lose herself entirely in its echoing silence. Someday perhaps. But now she veered toward home.

When she reached the clearing of the homestead, she rested her hands on her knees, waiting for her breathing to slow. There stood her ma's house, one room built of wood, shutters wide open in the summer afternoon, fir boughs on the roof turning brown. Dotting the small clearing were five other houses, built by her big brothers for their own families. Everywhere children wrestled and shrieked and chased. The whole place bustled, motion constant, the family like a huge beast with a thousand parts.

Rin spotted Ma, a sobbing grandchild on her hip and a long wooden spoon in her hand. Rin's mother was nearly as wide as she was tall and looked sturdy enough to face down a root-ripping storm.

"Brun, your Lila there is making a ruckus that'll scare the squirrels into winter," she shouted as she crossed the clearing, sounding loving even as she scolded. "See to her or I will. Gren, don't you knock over that pot I just filled if you want to live to supper! Jef, you sack of bones, get back to work. I didn't raise you to nap like an overfed piglet. Look at you children—what pretty needle-chains you made! Now don't go scratching each other's eyeballs. Tabi, let go of your brother! He's not a branch to swing from."

Rin followed Ma through the clearing and to the fire pit on the far side of the little house. When Ma began to stir the pot hanging over the fire, Rin took the spoon from her hand.

"Rin, there's my girl, only sensible person for leagues. Keep the stew from burning while I patch up Yuli's knee, will you? I can't think what those children meant by . . . now wait just a minute." Ma peered at Rin's face. "What's wrong?"

Rin tried to smile. "Nothing, Ma."

Ma sat Yuli on a bench, his sobbing more habitual than urgent, and put a hand under Rin's jaw. "You sure? You've been quiet lately . . . but it's not so much the quiet as something inside the quiet."

Rin shrugged, though her insides were turning to ice. Had Ma noticed these last months how often Rin ran off? Could Ma see that she was shaking inside? Would she speak the words, would she pronounce the problem and then make it right?

Ma felt her forehead, her cheeks, made her stick out her tongue, prodded her belly, listened to her elbows for creaks, pulled down her earflaps to look for rash. "Seem fine. You not feeling fine?"

Rin shrugged again. She'd never bothered anyone about the spiny things in her heart. It did not seem right to complain, especially not to Ma, who worked from the moment her eyes opened until she groaned as she lay down at night. Maybe everyone felt knotted like that but it just was not something spoken aloud. Or maybe only Rin was all wrong. If so, she'd never speak it, especially not to Ma.

"Could you . . ." Rin stopped.

"Ask me, Rinna." Her mother rarely told her what to do. Rin was the child who never needed scolding, who heard what her mother wanted before she'd even finished speaking. But Ma commanded her now, with fists on hips and eyes almost angry, daring her daughter to stay quiet. "Ask me."

And so Rin was surprised into saying exactly what she was thinking. "Could you hug me?"

Without hesitation, Ma pulled her in close, hugged her as if she were a tiny baby scared to be in the open world. Rin's head pressed into her mother's warm shoulder, and she breathed in wood smoke and juniper.

"My girl," Ma mumbled against her daughter's head. "My treasure. My perfect girl. How I love you and love you."

Rin wished she were six and could fit on her mother's lap, and every bad feeling or big scary terror could be drowned out by that ferocious love. There inside her arms, Rin's ache soothed a bit, but the snarled unease did not untangle. Rin had not believed one embrace could fix what was wrong, but she'd hoped enough to try.

"Thanks," she whispered.

Ma hugged her firmer still and smattered her head with kisses before letting go and returning to Yuli, whose cry had become offended.

"Anytime you want a hug, my treasure, you just blink," Ma said over her shoulder as she wiped Yuli's knee with a wet cloth and gave him a heel of bread to chew. "Can't think what's the matter with me if my little girl has to ask for love."

"I'm all right," Rin said, eager to hide it again. "Maybe I'm just feeling lonely for Razo."

"Yes, I bet that's it. That'll be it."

Rin scraped the bottom of the pot to keep the stew from

burning and tried to lose her worries by concentrating on the sounds around her—Yuli's shaky breaths, Ma's comforting mumbles, someone chopping wood, hollers from the children's game of owl and mouse. And the constant murmuring of the trees—wind in the high branches, pine needles clicking together, the soft knocks of cones, the creak of wood. But she could not shy away from the same thoughts grinding in her head: *hide yourself, try not to be who you are, you don't belong in this good family, even the trees think you're all wrong, you've got to go away, away.*

But where would she go?

In the yard everything quieted, then silence burst with hollers and calls of greeting. Could it be Wilem? He had not returned to the homestead since that night four months ago. Many times when she'd been running, Rin had almost turned toward his home. For what purpose? She did not understand why she'd felt so desperate for him to kiss her or why the trees now kept their peace to themselves. But surely nothing she could say could fix it.

Rin tiptoed around the side of the house. In her nervousness, her hands rose to cover her mouth.

A couple dozen members of her family gathered, her Ma squealing and administering hugs. In that sea of dark heads, Rin caught sight of orange. Her heart beat harder. There was only one person in all of Bayern with hair that color—Dasha, the ambassador from the country of Tira, and her brother Razo's girl. That meant Razo was here too.

Rin could hear Dasha saying, "It is a pleasure to return to the homestead again, Mistress Agget."

The Tiran girl had taken to referring to Ma as Mistress Agget, a formality that actually made Ma blush. All the folk known as Agget-kin called her Ma, including her grandchildren, who referred to their own mothers as "my ma" to avoid confusion. Even the nearest neighbors called her Ma. Only Dasha would stiffen things up like that. Apparently she was wealthy, her home in Tira a palace. "Isn't it wonderful how she's so comfortable here too?" Rin's family often said. But early last spring when Dasha had first arrived at the homestead, Rin had detected shock in Dasha's expression, even a little disdain. So why had Dasha stayed with Razo? That was what Rin wanted to know.

At last she glimpsed her brother, just exiting his mother's embrace. Razo looked the same—he was the youngest and shortest of the brothers, his cropped dark hair sticking straight up. Just the sight of him made her want to giggle. He was her best friend. And she had been his best friend—until Dasha.

Rin smiled, straightened, and waited for Razo to look for her, because he always did. She was usually standing a ways back, and he would call her Rinna-girl and push everyone aside to hug her or wrestle her or challenge her to a race or just knock his forehead against hers and smile.

His glance was roving. Her stomach tingled in anticipation. Then their eyes met, and in that moment before he could speak, a shock split her as she realized, *I can't tell him either.*

All these months she'd been planning what she would say on his return. "Razo, how can you stand to be away from the trees in the city? Or don't you feel anything from them? I used to think with them, through them, and feel calm. But not anymore." If she said that much, she'd also have to explain. "But then I kissed Wilem, and the trees changed toward me. I must be really bad if even the trees want me gone, and maybe if Ma knew me inside instead of out, she wouldn't love her girl anymore." If she could explain, perhaps he could help her make sense of it and fix it.

Only now did she understand that she could not admit it, even to him. He would not know how to mend her or the trees, and she could not reveal her secret ugliness, not without the risk of losing his love. That comprehension knocked her as if she'd fallen back-first out of a tree.

Razo waved. "Rinna-girl!"

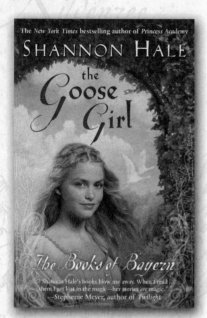

★ "A magical retelling of the Grimms' fairy tale. . . . Hale's retelling is a wonderfully rich one, full of eloquent description and lovely imagery. . . . Fans of high fantasy will be delighted with this novel."
—*SLJ*, starred review

"Enchanting. . . . A beautiful coming-of-age story."
—*The New York Times Book Review*

"Powerful and romantic."
—*Kirkus Reviews*

"This novel's pulsing heart lies in rich writing and sharply drawn characters, elements that will be devoured by genre fans just like kindling beneath flames."
—*Booklist*

★ "[A] stirring, stand-alone adventure. . . . Suspenseful, magical, and heartfelt, this is a story that will wholly envelop its readers."
—*Booklist*, starred review

★ "This novel will be a special treat for readers of Hale's other two companion books, but it also stands on its own as a unique and tender coming-of-age story."
—*Publishers Weekly*, starred review

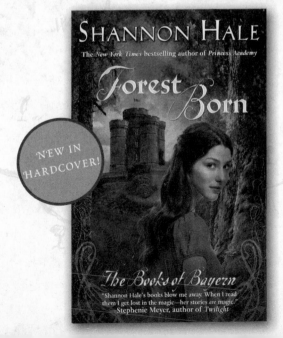

Eager for more tales of magic and adventure?

Follow Rapunzel and Jack
(of "Jack and the beanstalk" fame) to
new lands in Shannon Hale's graphic novels!

BLOOMSBURY

www.bloomsburyusa.com
www.shannonhale.com